I0714430

PALOMAR CITY
THE LOCKS
NORTHLAND
PALOMAR GENERAL HOSPITAL
Rivertown
City Hall
The Docks
D16
D14
D01
D08
Palomar General
D04
D02
D05
D12
D15
D06
D12 Annex
D03
D10
D07
D13
EAST HARBOR
D11
Star Lucky Kitchen
D19
D20
THE BREAKS
D17
D18
CITY ISLAND
= CITY DISTRICT
= INDEPENDENT DISTRICT
2 MILES
THE GATECRASHERS

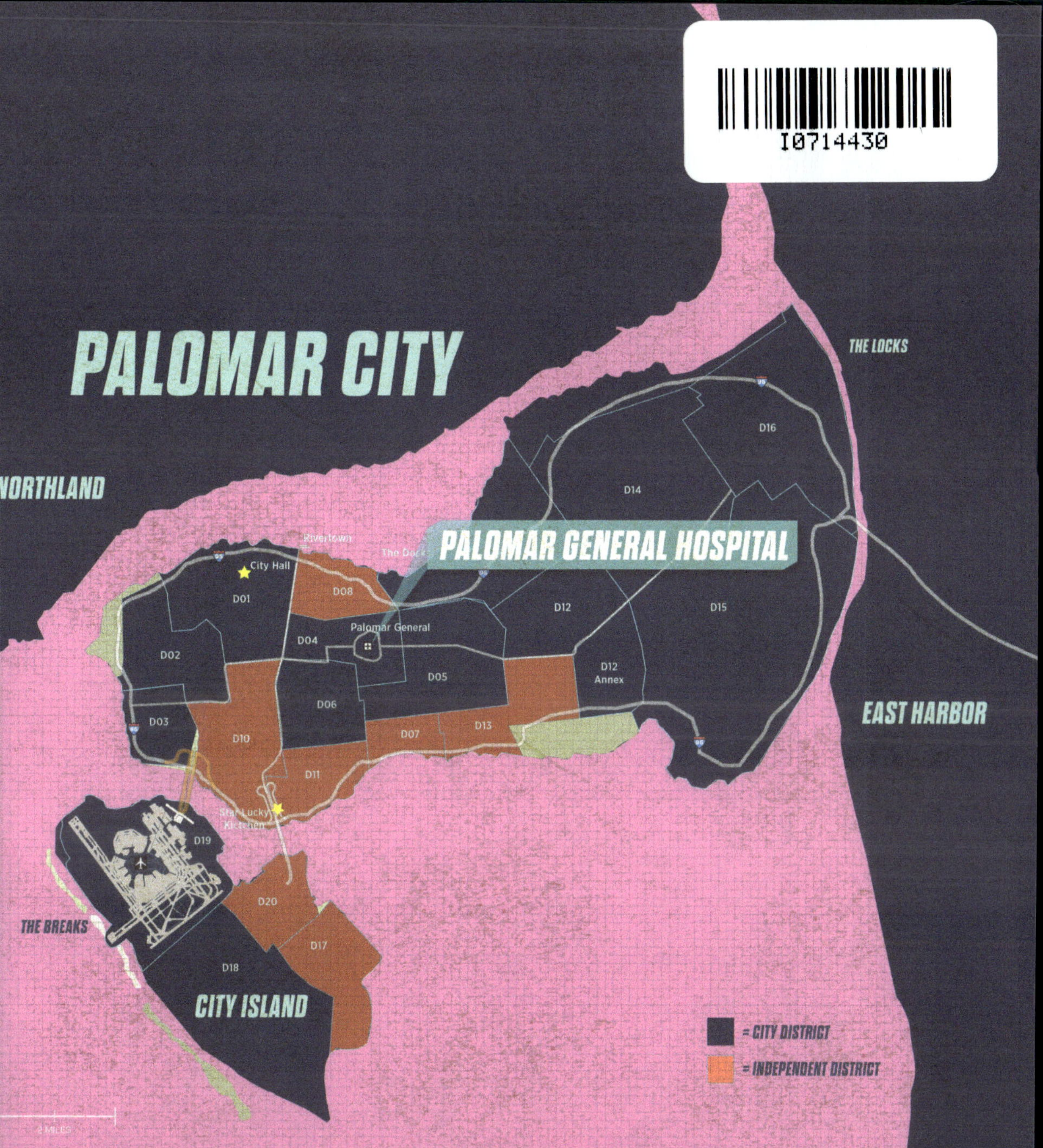

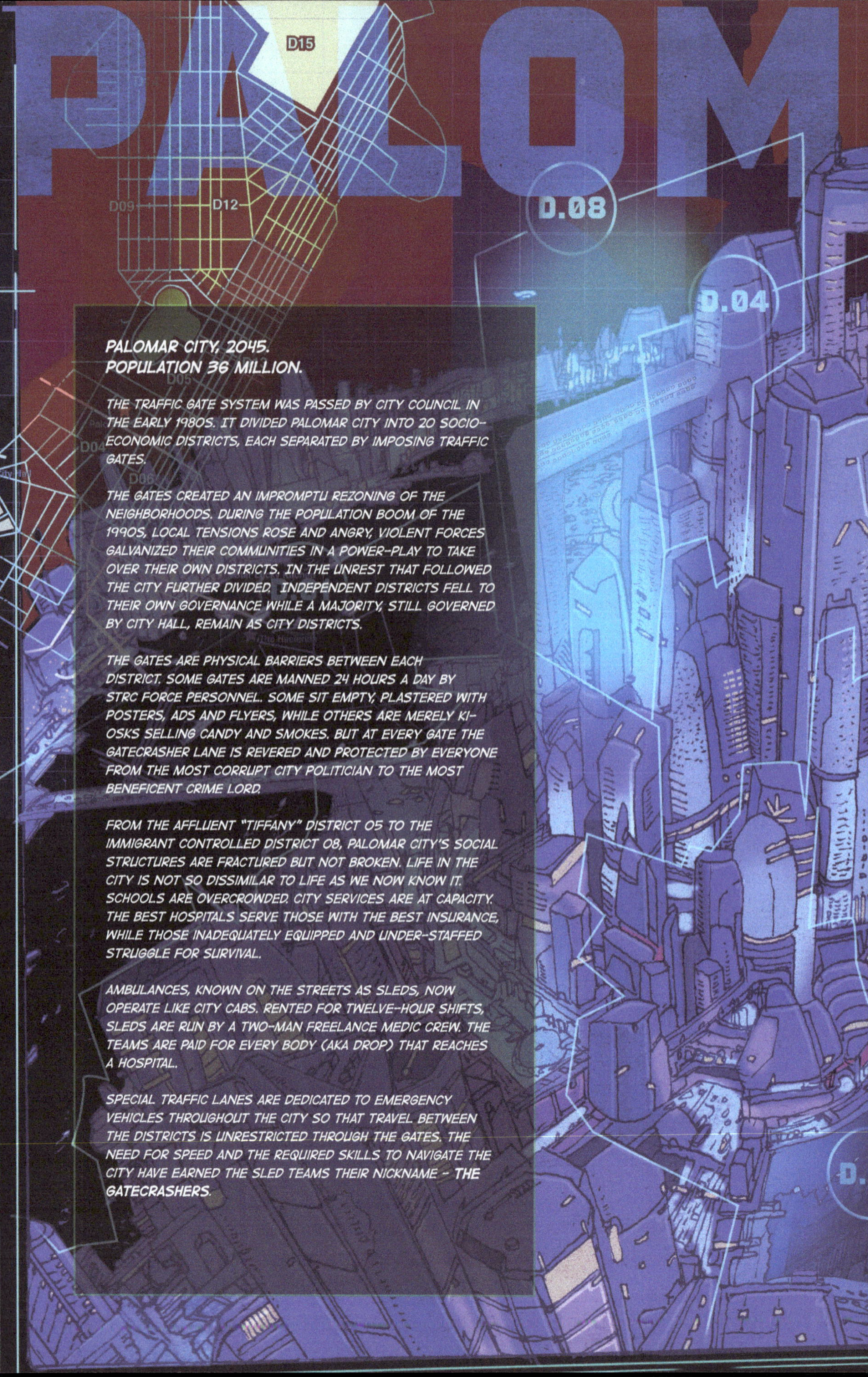

PALOM
D15
D09
D12
D.08
D.04
D05
D04
D06

PALOMAR CITY, 2045.
POPULATION 36 MILLION.

THE TRAFFIC GATE SYSTEM WAS PASSED BY CITY COUNCIL IN
THE EARLY 1980S. IT DIVIDED PALOMAR CITY INTO 20 SOCIO-
ECONOMIC DISTRICTS, EACH SEPARATED BY IMPOSING TRAFFIC
GATES.

THE GATES CREATED AN IMPROMPTU REZONING OF THE
NEIGHBORHOODS. DURING THE POPULATION BOOM OF THE
1990S, LOCAL TENSIONS ROSE AND ANGRY, VIOLENT FORCES
GALVANIZED THEIR COMMUNITIES IN A POWER-PLAY TO TAKE
OVER THEIR OWN DISTRICTS. IN THE UNREST THAT FOLLOWED
THE CITY FURTHER DIVIDED. INDEPENDENT DISTRICTS FELL TO
THEIR OWN GOVERNANCE WHILE A MAJORITY, STILL GOVERNED
BY CITY HALL, REMAIN AS CITY DISTRICTS.

THE GATES ARE PHYSICAL BARRIERS BETWEEN EACH
DISTRICT. SOME GATES ARE MANNED 24 HOURS A DAY BY
STRC FORCE PERSONNEL. SOME SIT EMPTY, PLASTERED WITH
POSTERS, ADS AND FLYERS, WHILE OTHERS ARE MERELY KI-
OSKS SELLING CANDY AND SMOKES. BUT AT EVERY GATE THE
GATECRASHER LANE IS REVERED AND PROTECTED BY EVERYONE
FROM THE MOST CORRUPT CITY POLITICIAN TO THE MOST
BENEFICENT CRIME LORD.

FROM THE AFFLUENT "TIFFANY" DISTRICT 05 TO THE
IMMIGRANT CONTROLLED DISTRICT 08, PALOMAR CITY'S SOCIAL
STRUCTURES ARE FRACTURED BUT NOT BROKEN. LIFE IN THE
CITY IS NOT SO DISSIMILAR TO LIFE AS WE NOW KNOW IT.
SCHOOLS ARE OVERCROWDED. CITY SERVICES ARE AT CAPACITY.
THE BEST HOSPITALS SERVE THOSE WITH THE BEST INSURANCE,
WHILE THOSE INADEQUATELY EQUIPPED AND UNDER-STAFFED
STRUGGLE FOR SURVIVAL.

AMBULANCES, KNOWN ON THE STREETS AS SLEDS, NOW
OPERATE LIKE CITY CABS. RENTED FOR TWELVE-HOUR SHIFTS,
SLEDS ARE RUN BY A TWO-MAN FREELANCE MEDIC CREW. THE
TEAMS ARE PAID FOR EVERY BODY (AKA DROP) THAT REACHES
A HOSPITAL.

SPECIAL TRAFFIC LANES ARE DEDICATED TO EMERGENCY
VEHICLES THROUGHOUT THE CITY SO THAT TRAVEL BETWEEN
THE DISTRICTS IS UNRESTRICTED THROUGH THE GATES. THE
NEED FOR SPEED AND THE REQUIRED SKILLS TO NAVIGATE THE
CITY HAVE EARNED THE SLED TEAMS THEIR NICKNAME - THE
GATECRASHERS.

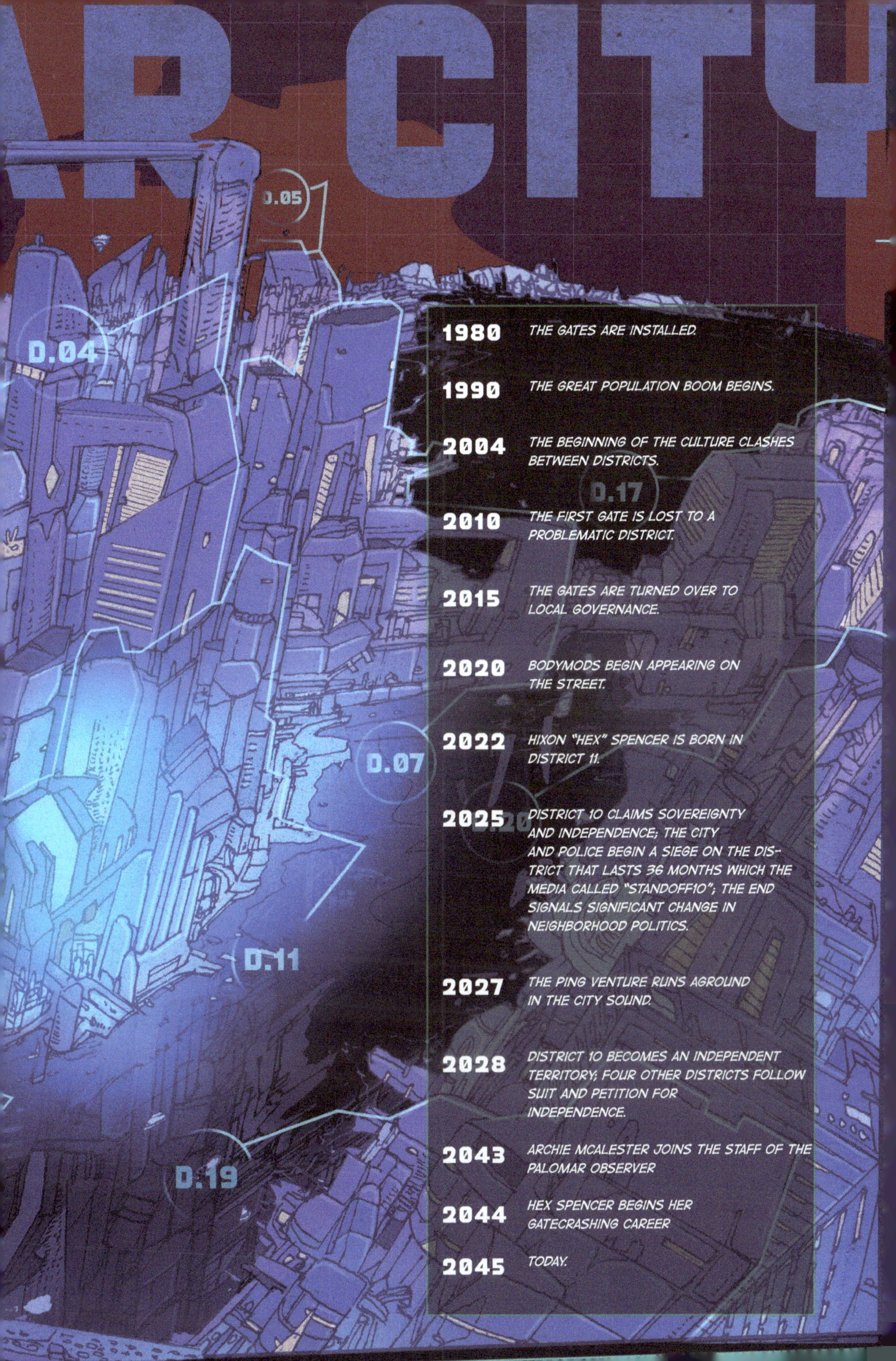

D.05

D.04

D.17

D.07

D.11

D.19

1980	THE GATES ARE INSTALLED.
1990	THE GREAT POPULATION BOOM BEGINS.
2004	THE BEGINNING OF THE CULTURE CLASHES BETWEEN DISTRICTS.
2010	THE FIRST GATE IS LOST TO A PROBLEMATIC DISTRICT.
2015	THE GATES ARE TURNED OVER TO LOCAL GOVERNANCE.
2020	BODYMODS BEGIN APPEARING ON THE STREET.
2022	HIXON "HEX" SPENCER IS BORN IN DISTRICT 11.
2025	DISTRICT 10 CLAIMS SOVEREIGNTY AND INDEPENDENCE; THE CITY AND POLICE BEGIN A SIEGE ON THE DISTRICT THAT LASTS 36 MONTHS WHICH THE MEDIA CALLED "STANDOFF10"; THE END SIGNALS SIGNIFICANT CHANGE IN NEIGHBORHOOD POLITICS.
2027	THE PING VENTURE RUNS AGROUND IN THE CITY SOUND.
2028	DISTRICT 10 BECOMES AN INDEPENDENT TERRITORY; FOUR OTHER DISTRICTS FOLLOW SUIT AND PETITION FOR INDEPENDENCE.
2043	ARCHIE MCALESTER JOINS THE STAFF OF THE PALOMAR OBSERVER
2044	HEX SPENCER BEGINS HER GATECRASHING CAREER
2045	TODAY.

PALOMAR GENERAL EDITION

WRITTEN BY	ARTIST	EDITOR	CONSULTING EDITOR
ZACHARY MORTENSEN	SUTU	DIANA WILLIAMS	MARK HAYNES

ghostrobot

Zachary Mortener - Exec Producer
Mark DePace - Exec Producer
Made In New York City, USA
www.GhostRobot.com

THE GATECRASHERS GRAPHIC NOVEL 001
"A Night of Gatecrashing"

ISBN 978-0-9904755-2-1

Copyright © 2013 by Zachary Mortensen

All rights reserved.

No part of this book may be reproduced in any form or by any electronic or mechanical means including information storage and retrieval systems, without permission in writing from the author. The only exception is by a reviewer, who may quote short excerpts in a review.

Printed in the United States of America
Released Digitally October 2014
First Printing: October 2014
The Gatecrashers Story Number: 001.004.01

ghostrobot

GATE 06
EMERGENCY
TOLL
C-17
C-11

GATE 06
CIVILIAN GATE
SAM, IT'S HEX, THANKS AGAIN FOR THE EARLY SHIFT CHANGE, I OWE YOU ONE.
GO OUT FOR DRINKS WITH ME.
HONK
HONK
DROP IT SAM, NOT GONNA HAPPEN.
SMACK!
OK HEX – WHAT'D YOU NEED A SLED FOR WITH NO PARTNER?
HONK
NONE OF YOUR BUSINESS.
0770
I'D HATE TO HAVE TO REPORT THAT TO RADA.
HONK
HONK
TRAFFIC DELAYS
REPORT ANYTHING AND IT'LL BE THE LAST NIGHT YOU CAN USE THOSE HANDS TO SPANK-IT TO THE PICTURES YOU KEEP TAKING OF ME IN THE GARAGE.
'CLICK'

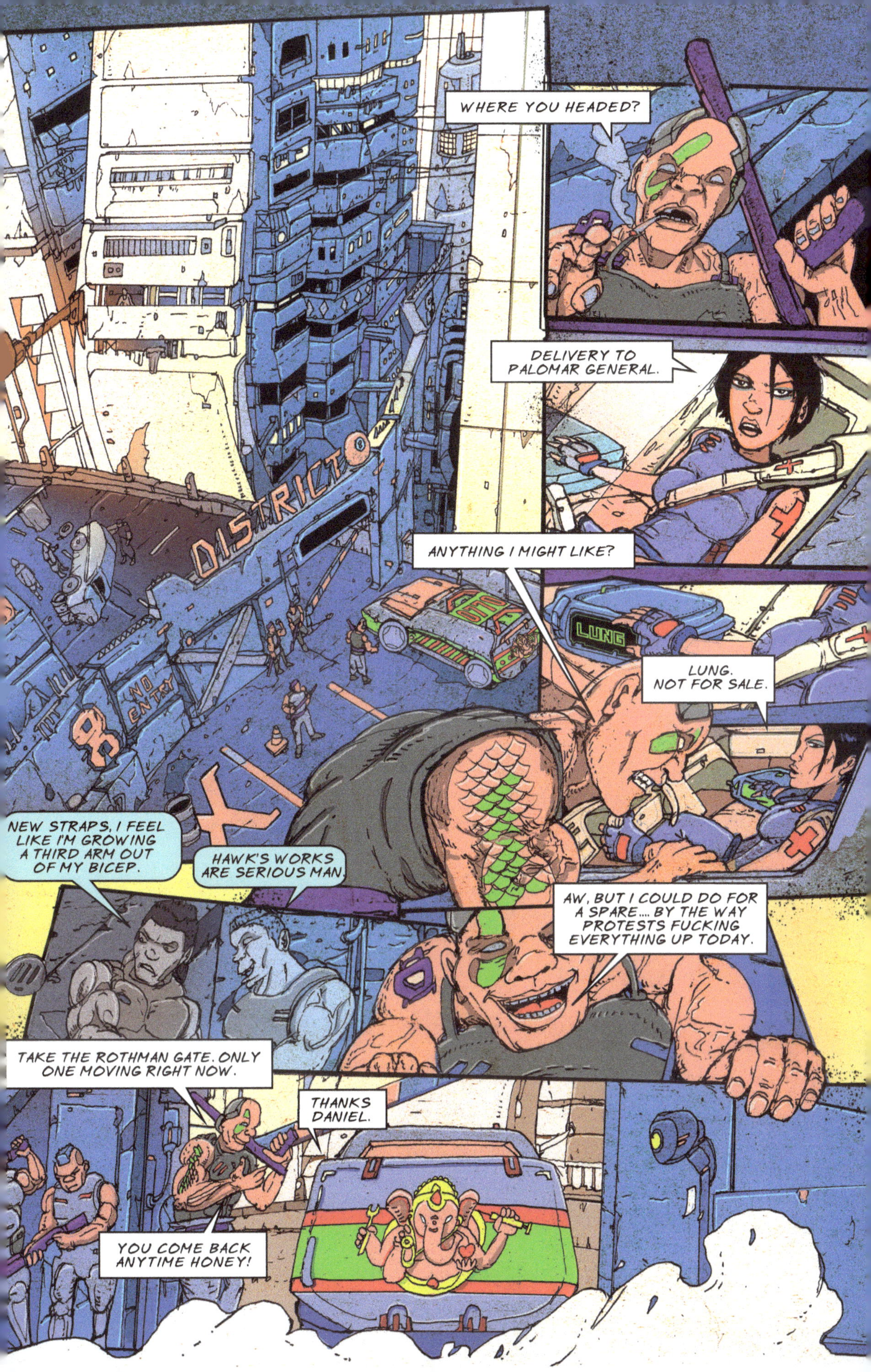

WHERE YOU HEADED?
DELIVERY TO PALOMAR GENERAL.
ANYTHING I MIGHT LIKE?
LUNG. NOT FOR SALE.
NEW STRAPS, I FEEL LIKE I'M GROWING A THIRD ARM OUT OF MY BICEP.
HAWK'S WORKS ARE SERIOUS MAN.
AW, BUT I COULD DO FOR A SPARE.... BY THE WAY PROTESTS FUCKING EVERYTHING UP TODAY.
TAKE THE ROTHMAN GATE. ONLY ONE MOVING RIGHT NOW.
THANKS DANIEL.
YOU COME BACK ANYTIME HONEY!

THIS IS CHARLOTTE PAYNE ON ACTION 77 NEWS. FOR SIX WEEKS THE TOP NEWS STORY IN PALOMAR CITY CONTINUES TO BE THE PROTESTS IN INDEPENDENT DISTRICT EIGHT. AS ISOLATED EPISODES OF VIOLENCE ARE ON THE RISE, NEITHER SIDE IS BACKING DOWN.
WITH THE CITY'S DECISION TO ANNEX FOUR SQUARE BLOCKS IN SUPPORT OF UBER-DEVELOPER, DANE BRENNAN'S LUXURY-SKYSCRAPER PROJECT...
HUNDREDS OF RESIDENTS HAVE TAKEN TO THE TOP OF THE ROTHMAN SKYWAY IN PROTEST. IN RECENT DAYS THE CITY POLICE RESPONSE HAS DOUBLED AT THE FRONT LINE NEAR THE DISTRICT ONE BORDER.
MUMS FOR DISTRICT 8

THE OBSERVER
PALOMAR CITY
Edition Final

VIOLENCE ERUPTS IN D.08

At least 12 protestors were sent to area hospitals on Thursday evening amid heightened violence that broke past the security and show lines on the Skyway over District 08. One Palomar Observer reporter was caught in the clash of a particularly angry crowd. He was thrown to the ground, beaten and his broadcasters works were torn from his head. He suffered serious injury. He is in Palomar official hospital in serious condition.

Reports of violence are as the D08 Committee states "The spontaneous acts of violence are caused by agitators. These incidents are not official...

EXCUSE ME! ELIZABETH.

I'VE GOT A SCOOP ON THE SKYWAY. YOU'VE GOTTA LET ME WRITE IT!

ARCHIE! THE ANSWER IS STILL NO!

DID YOU HEAR WHAT HAPPENED TO DALE?

EVEN WITH A PRESS BADGE THEY RIPPED OUT HIS BROADCASTERS AND HE ALMOST LOST THE EYE. 20 YEARS IN THE FIELD.

YOUR FATHER WOULD KILL ME IF THAT HAPPENED TO YOU.

AND WHAT ABOUT DALE? WE BOTH KNOW HIS BROADCASTERS ARE ALREADY ON THE BLACK MARKET. THAT'S A CRIME AND THAT'S A STORY. WE COULD DO AN EXPOSE PIECE FOLLOWING HIS WETWORK.

WE'RE PULLING OBSERVER PERSONNEL BACK TO CITY DISTRICT FOUR TO COVER THE PROTEST REMOTELY.

COVER IT REMOTELY!?!

NOT YOU

SEE MARION ON THE CITY DESK. HE'S GOT A LIFESTYLE PIECE HE NEEDS A REPORTER ON.

MEDIA
DALE CABEZA

AWESOME. YEAR TWO OF WRITING CITY DESK FILLER CONTENT.

Release goes on to say that the committee feels like the City and Developer negotiations are sliding off the table and they to get farther from the original any suitable offer.

...ce with D08 leaders in a closed session today and parties close to the negotiations said that tempers had smoothed by the end of the meeting. Unofficial word is that there could be a compromise and agreement in place as early as monday. This would end 8 straight escalating...

STUDENT: MELITA, – LESSON RECORDING – MODELING FLUID DYNAMICS WITH THE PRESENCE OF A DISPERSED PHASE IN THE FORM OF NON-SPHERICAL PARTICLES.
HEX YOU'RE HOME?
I'VE GOT AN HOUR BEFORE I NEED TO BE AT DISPATCH. HOW'S YOUR HOMEWORK COMING ALONG?
DONE, I'M GOING OVER TO VIOLET'S TONIGHT.
WE'VE BEEN OVER THIS.
YOU DON'T HAVE A DISTRICT TRANSFER ID.
I DON'T NEED ONE.
YOU'RE 13, YOU NEED ONE.
I PICKED UP DINNER!
HA HAHA. SPICY PIM FROM D4!
BRIBES WON'T WORK
NOT EVEN YOUR FAVORITE MEAL?
NO THANKS I HAD LUNG FOR LUNCH
I'M GOING TO VIOLET'S
NO MELITA, YOU'RE NOT!
LUNG TRANSPLANT FOR D.06
MONA'S CLOTHES

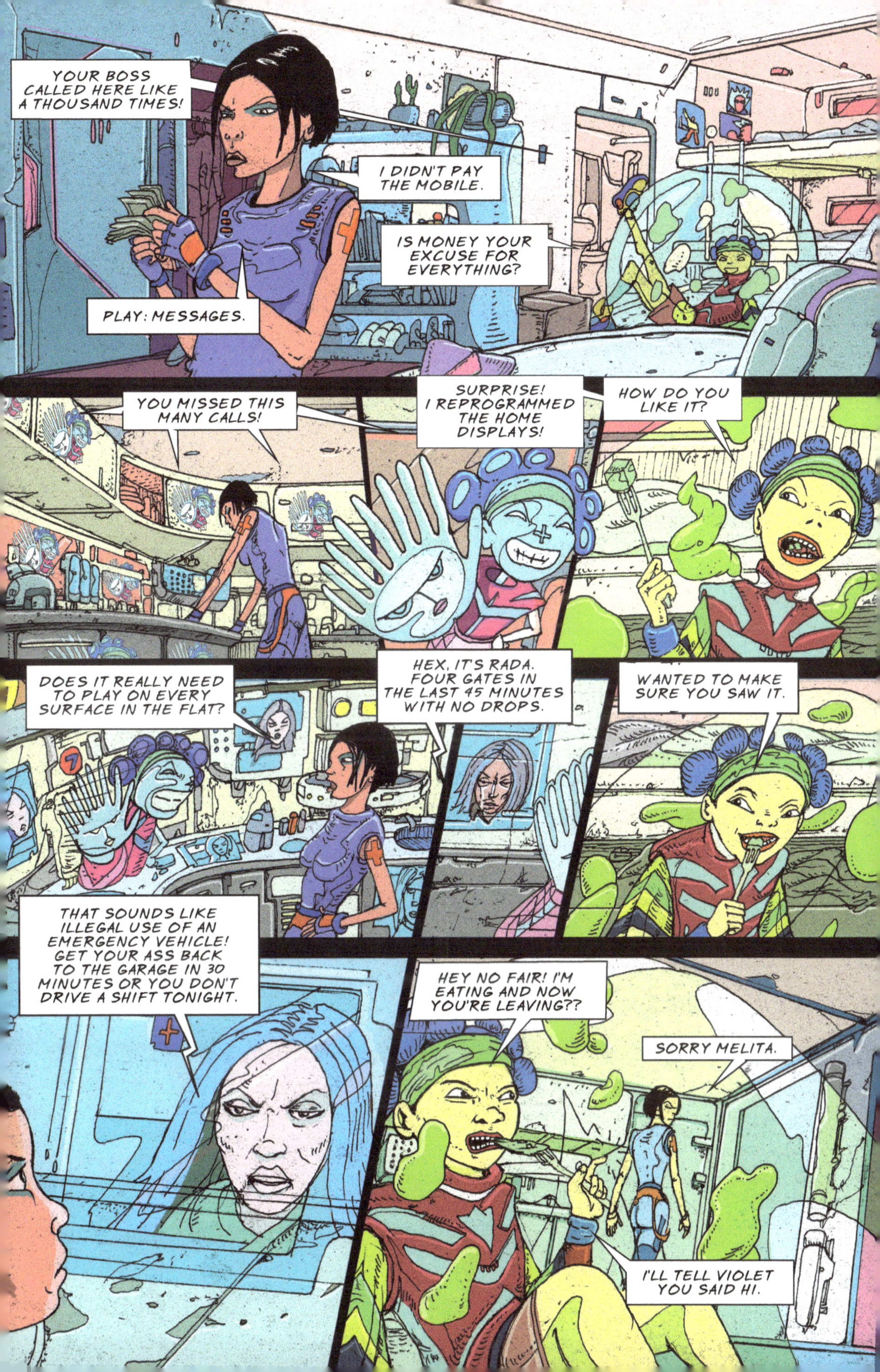

YOUR BOSS CALLED HERE LIKE A THOUSAND TIMES!
I DIDN'T PAY THE MOBILE.
IS MONEY YOUR EXCUSE FOR EVERYTHING?
PLAY: MESSAGES.
YOU MISSED THIS MANY CALLS!
SURPRISE! I REPROGRAMMED THE HOME DISPLAYS!
HOW DO YOU LIKE IT?
DOES IT REALLY NEED TO PLAY ON EVERY SURFACE IN THE FLAT?
HEX, IT'S RADA. FOUR GATES IN THE LAST 45 MINUTES WITH NO DROPS.
WANTED TO MAKE SURE YOU SAW IT.
THAT SOUNDS LIKE ILLEGAL USE OF AN EMERGENCY VEHICLE! GET YOUR ASS BACK TO THE GARAGE IN 30 MINUTES OR YOU DON'T DRIVE A SHIFT TONIGHT.
HEY NO FAIR! I'M EATING AND NOW YOU'RE LEAVING??
SORRY MELITA.
I'LL TELL VIOLET YOU SAID HI.

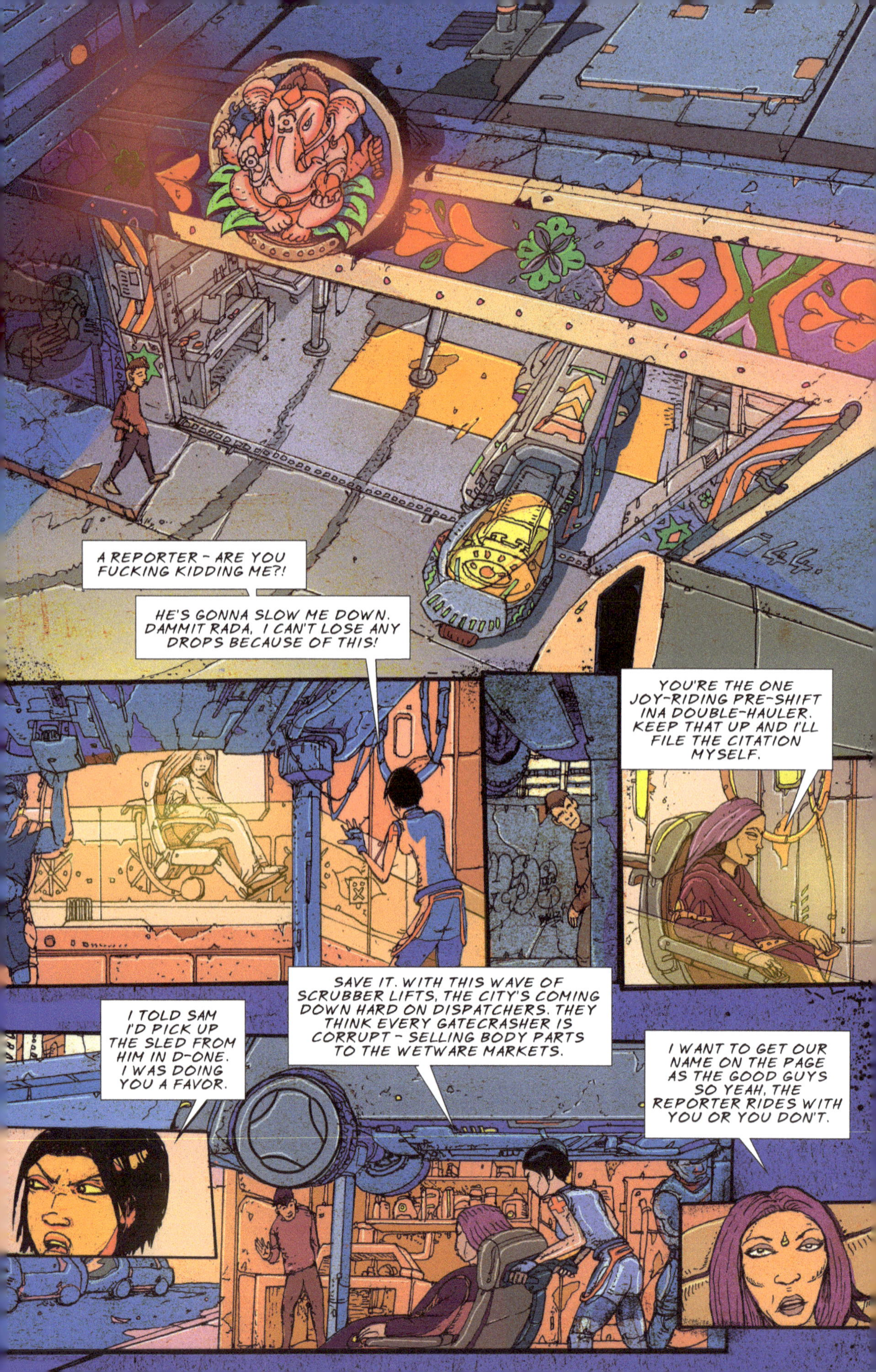

A REPORTER - ARE YOU FUCKING KIDDING ME?!
HE'S GONNA SLOW ME DOWN. DAMMIT RADA, I CAN'T LOSE ANY DROPS BECAUSE OF THIS!
YOU'RE THE ONE JOY-RIDING PRE-SHIFT INA DOUBLE-HAULER. KEEP THAT UP AND I'LL FILE THE CITATION MYSELF.
SAVE IT. WITH THIS WAVE OF SCRUBBER LIFTS, THE CITY'S COMING DOWN HARD ON DISPATCHERS. THEY THINK EVERY GATECRASHER IS CORRUPT - SELLING BODY PARTS TO THE WETWARE MARKETS.
I TOLD SAM I'D PICK UP THE SLED FROM HIM IN D-ONE. I WAS DOING YOU A FAVOR.
I WANT TO GET OUR NAME ON THE PAGE AS THE GOOD GUYS SO YEAH, THE REPORTER RIDES WITH YOU OR YOU DON'T.

THAT'S HIM?
AWW HE'S CUTE. HOW'S ABOUT SCRATCHING HIS BELLY AND SEE IF HE ROLLS OVER FOR YOU?
HEY.
I'M ARCHIE, NICE TO MEET...
MEET ME AT STAR LUCKY IN 30. WE LEAVE FROM THERE.
VERY SMOOTH
AND SHE'S OUT OF HERE
WHY DON'T YOU DO A STORY ON THIS?
SHORT STORY!
SHE'S GOT A BIT OF A TEMPER BUT SHE'S GOOD AT WHAT SHE DOES. KEEPS HER HEAD DOWN, HER SLED CLEAN AND BRINGS IN AT LEAST FIVE DROPS A NIGHT, EVERY NIGHT.
SHE'S ALWAYS GOT THE SLED-RENT AND NEVER COMPLAINS
WELL HARDLY EVER.

CHECK YOUR VITALS
EXCUSE ME MISTER BRENNAN.
NOT NOW JACQUI
YOUR HEART RATE'S GOING UP!
HEART RATE

INITIATE TODAY
TIME TO WRAP UP. IT'S ON. TODAY.
YOU SHOULD GET SHOWERED AND CHANGED.
AND JACQUI...
FIND ME A NEW TRAINER. PREFERABLY ONE THAT CAN GO A FULL 12 ROUNDS.

MEDICAL +
SAY NO
LEGAL DEPT
PROPAGANDA
RESIST ANNEX
KRAZ I WAS LOOKING FOR YOU? WE STILL GOING TO THE RALLY?
NAH MAN, GOT SOMETHING MORE IMPORTANT..
ALL THREE OF YOU? NEED A HAND?
OUR STREETS DOCKS DISTRICT
Find out your right
WHERE: 1st Floor Commi-
TIME: 8:00 PM
NO WE DON'T.
DON'T SWEAT IT. I'LL COME ALONG.
IGNORE HIM, KEEP MOVING.
BUZZ OFF DUDE.
THATCH, WE DON'T NEED HELP. DON'T FOLLOW US.
I'M PART OF THE TEAM!
YOU'RE STILL NOT PART OF THE TEAM.
Must attend for any Front Line protestors.
what City Police can and can't do in an Inde
rn what to do if you ar
City District and what extradition
district Citizens have.
NO ANNEX

POSITIVE. 狗屁

DESTINATION: MR. KAN
FOREVER
DISTRICT

TWO PAYMENTS?
JUST ONE.
YOU'RE STILL TWO BEHIND.
MR. RUFFO WANTS TO TALK TO YOU.
I HAVE TO GO TO WORK.
DON'T WORRY. HE'LL CALL YOU WHEN HE'S READY.
TWO PAYMENTS. NO GOOD.
Star Lucky Kitchen
D10

THE PROPRIETORS OF THE STAR LUCKY KITCHEN WERE CLEARLY NOT CATERING TO A 'WALK-IN' CROWD.
GYOZA

THE OBSERVER

DISTRICT FOOD FOCUS

by Pauline Platt

The Star Lucky Kitchen parking lot is a steel-grated platform thirty-meters wide suspended fifteen stories above the city on the underside of the South River Bridge. The platform, long unused, was originally built for maintenance vehicles. It became a popular spot for local Gatecrashers to switch shifts without having to drive back to their dispatch garages. One cold, rainy evening an enterprising food cart vendor, who goes only by the name Lucky Elvis, pushed his small cart out the long expanse of the bridge and down the maintenance ramp to the underslung parking area. The rest is history.

Today the Star Lucky Kitchen has grown from that original cart into a semi-permanent structure built off of the stone anchorage of the bridge itself. Star Lucky has a five-meter stainless steel countertop running chest-high across an open kitchen window where Lucky Elvis still personally serves an all PIM menu with eight of the spiciest curries in the city. The Star Lucky is also a licensed dispensary. You can rub elbows with the Gatecrashers who grab a quick bite and restock their supplies from a selection that rivals any hospital in the city. The stock-master says they have everything from micro-dermal plasters to opioid analgesics -- up to control series 10 -- you name it, they've got it. Hopefully you won't need any of that if you're just here for the delicious street food.

2 HEMO-CANS OF A-POSITIVE AND O-NEG AND A CASE OF DERMI-PLAST.
HEY! CAN I HELP?
SPARKY?
'IT'S ARCHIE.
SURE, GIVE ME A HAND.

YOU PAY FOR SUPPLIES YOURSELF?
YEAH, DON'T PUT 'EM DOWN OR LET 'EM OUT OF YOUR SIGHT. SHIT DISAPPEARS FAST AROUND HERE.
TYPE A THAT'S MY TYPE.
LET'S HOPE WE DON'T HAVE TO USE IT ON YOU.
WAKE UP PUCK! I GOT YOU AN A-O SHAKE!
HEY SPARKY, YOU WANNA SIP OF THIS?
IS A-O THE DRINK OF CHOICE FOR THE GATE-CRASHER SET?
IT'S ARCHIE. I'VE SEEN IT AROUND, BUT NEVER TRIED IT.
NAH, JUST MY THING.
SO, YOU READY FOR SOME ACTION?
CAREFUL WITH THAT STUFF. IT'LL MESS YOU UP.

OUR CITY OUR DOCKS WE ARE DISTRICT 8
SAVE 8
FUCK THE CITY
8
K
ID. CONFIRMED
ID: KRAZ CONFIRMED
KRAZ ENGAGED TRACKER AND BROADCASTER BLOCKING.
NO DOCKS FOR $$$ SAVE DISTRICT 8!
DEVICE STILL WITH KRAZ.
DEVICE CONFIRMED

ZERO-SEVEN SEVENTY LOCK ON THE DROP FOXTROT-SIX-EIGHT-DELTA-TEN-BRAVO
55 YEAR OLD WHITE MALE COLLAPSED AFTER COMPLAINTS OF CHEST PAINS. CALL LOGGED AT 18:22. 25 HOWARD STREET, 24TH FLOOR. D-TEN
THEN AS IF TO PROVIDE SOME MEDITATIVE RELIEF FROM IT ALL – THERE IS A LITTLE PLASTIC BONSAI TREE MOUNTED ON THE DASH. HAS OUR TOUGH-AS-NAILS GATECRASHER GOT A SENSE OF HUMOR?
IF YOU THINK YOU'RE DOING PLAY BY PLAY COMMENTARY ALL NIGHT, I'M GOING TO HAVE PUCK TRANQUILIZE YOU.
SORRY JUST TAKING NOTES.
NEW NOTE TO SELF: WATCH OUT FOR PUCK.
I THINK THIS IS MY FIRST TIME IN DISTRICT 10.
NOW I GET IT, ALL BOOK SMARTS, NO STREET SMARTS.
DISTRICT 10
SPARKY, WE COULD PROBABLY GET YOU A BETTER HAIR-CUT AROUND HERE. SOMEWHERE.

SCREECH!!!...
LOAD FLOOR PLANS. NOTIFY LIFTS AND TAG EMERGENCY EXITS.
LOC: 25 HOWARD ST.
CALCULATING FASTEST ROUTE
STANDARD LUXURY APARTMENT. HEX AND PUCK RACE INTO ACTION CARRYING A SUPER-LIGHT GYRO-STRETCHER
IO APARTMENT
PATIENT LOC: LEVEL 24, RM.241
ELEVATOR AT FOYER

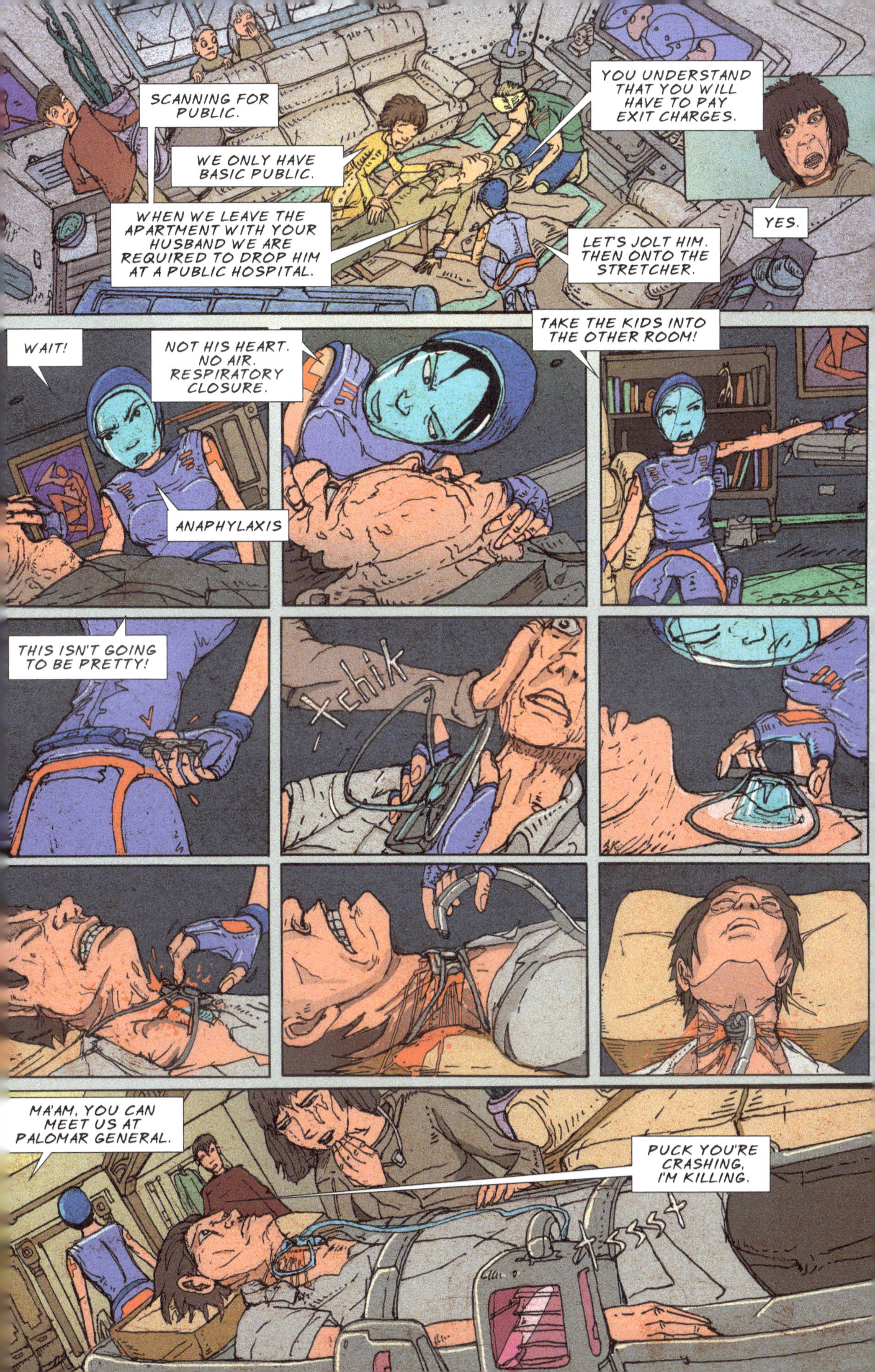

SCANNING FOR PUBLIC.
WE ONLY HAVE BASIC PUBLIC.
WHEN WE LEAVE THE APARTMENT WITH YOUR HUSBAND WE ARE REQUIRED TO DROP HIM AT A PUBLIC HOSPITAL.
YOU UNDERSTAND THAT YOU WILL HAVE TO PAY EXIT CHARGES.
YES.
LET'S JOLT HIM. THEN ONTO THE STRETCHER.
WAIT!
NOT HIS HEART. NO AIR. RESPIRATORY CLOSURE.
ANAPHYLAXIS
TAKE THE KIDS INTO THE OTHER ROOM!
THIS ISN'T GOING TO BE PRETTY!
xchik
MA'AM, YOU CAN MEET US AT PALOMAR GENERAL.
PUCK YOU'RE CRASHING, I'M KILLING.

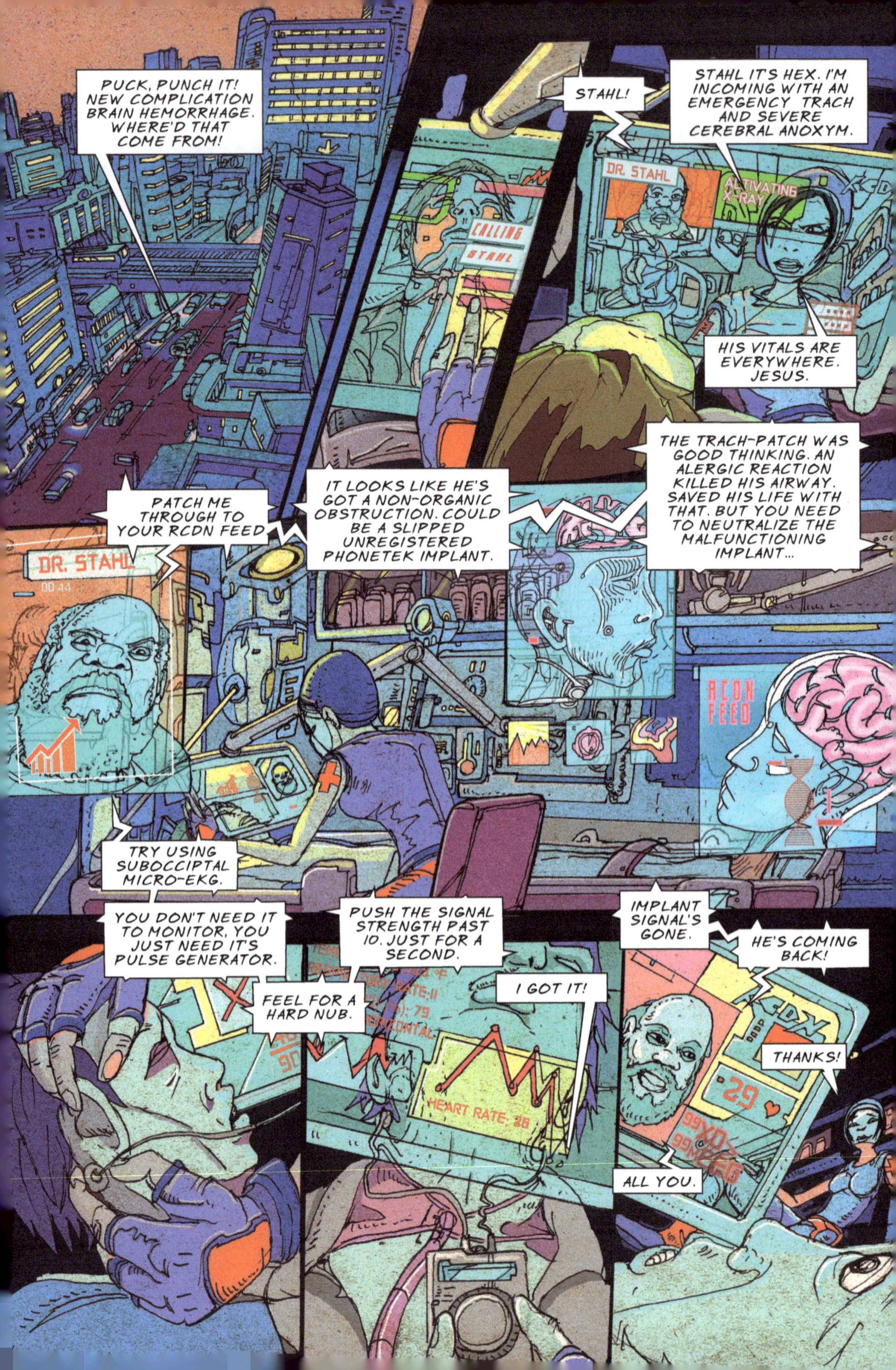

PUCK, PUNCH IT! NEW COMPLICATION BRAIN HEMORRHAGE. WHERE'D THAT COME FROM!
STAHL!
STAHL IT'S HEX. I'M INCOMING WITH AN EMERGENCY TRACH AND SEVERE CEREBRAL ANOXYM.
DR. STAHL
ALTIVATING X-RAY
CALLING STAHL
HIS VITALS ARE EVERYWHERE. JESUS.
THE TRACH-PATCH WAS GOOD THINKING. AN ALERGIC REACTION KILLED HIS AIRWAY. SAVED HIS LIFE WITH THAT. BUT YOU NEED TO NEUTRALIZE THE MALFUNCTIONING IMPLANT...
PATCH ME THROUGH TO YOUR RCDN FEED
IT LOOKS LIKE HE'S GOT A NON-ORGANIC OBSTRUCTION. COULD BE A SLIPPED UNREGISTERED PHONETEK IMPLANT.
DR. STAHL
00:44
RCDN FEED
TRY USING SUBOCCIPTAL MICRO-EKG.
YOU DON'T NEED IT TO MONITOR, YOU JUST NEED IT'S PULSE GENERATOR.
PUSH THE SIGNAL STRENGTH PAST 10. JUST FOR A SECOND.
IMPLANT SIGNAL'S GONE.
HE'S COMING BACK!
FEEL FOR A HARD NUB.
I GOT IT!
THANKS!
HEART RATE: 20
ALL YOU.

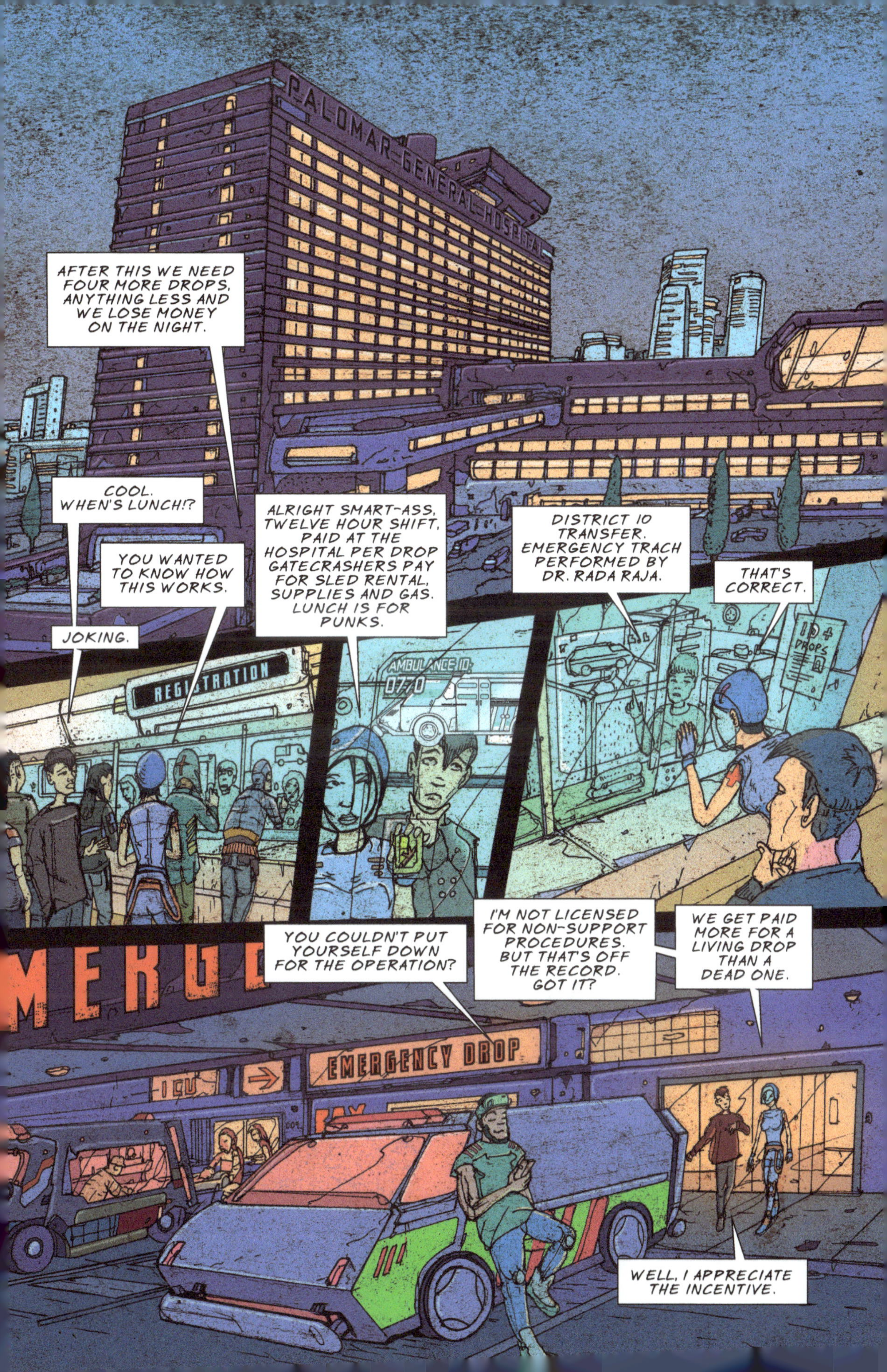

PALOMAR GENERAL HOSPITAL
AFTER THIS WE NEED FOUR MORE DROPS, ANYTHING LESS AND WE LOSE MONEY ON THE NIGHT.
COOL. WHEN'S LUNCH!?
YOU WANTED TO KNOW HOW THIS WORKS.
JOKING.
ALRIGHT SMART-ASS, TWELVE HOUR SHIFT, PAID AT THE HOSPITAL PER DROP GATECRASHERS PAY FOR SLED RENTAL, SUPPLIES AND GAS. LUNCH IS FOR PUNKS.
DISTRICT 10 TRANSFER. EMERGENCY TRACH PERFORMED BY DR. RADA RAJA.
THAT'S CORRECT.
REGISTRATION
AMBULANCE ID 077-0
ID 4 DROPS
YOU COULDN'T PUT YOURSELF DOWN FOR THE OPERATION?
I'M NOT LICENSED FOR NON-SUPPORT PROCEDURES. BUT THAT'S OFF THE RECORD. GOT IT?
WE GET PAID MORE FOR A LIVING DROP THAN A DEAD ONE.
MERC
EMERGENCY DROP
ICU
WELL, I APPRECIATE THE INCENTIVE.

THAT'S A TIGHT FIT. YOU GOING FOR THE METRO LOOK?
T-MINUS 11 MINUTES.
FUCK OFF KRAZ, YOU CAN GO IN COSTUME NEXT TIME.
LOSE NO GROUND BITCHES!
OR LOSE A LOT. HA!
I'M GOING BELOW TO MARK. YOU'RE ON YOUR OWN FROM HERE. MAKE IT COUNT.
LOSE NO
SAVE D8
SIM THE DOC
NO DOCK FOR
THE CITY CAN SAY NO TO THE CITY
INVADERS BACK YOUR OWN CITY!
OCCUPY GOTHHAM SKYWWAY!

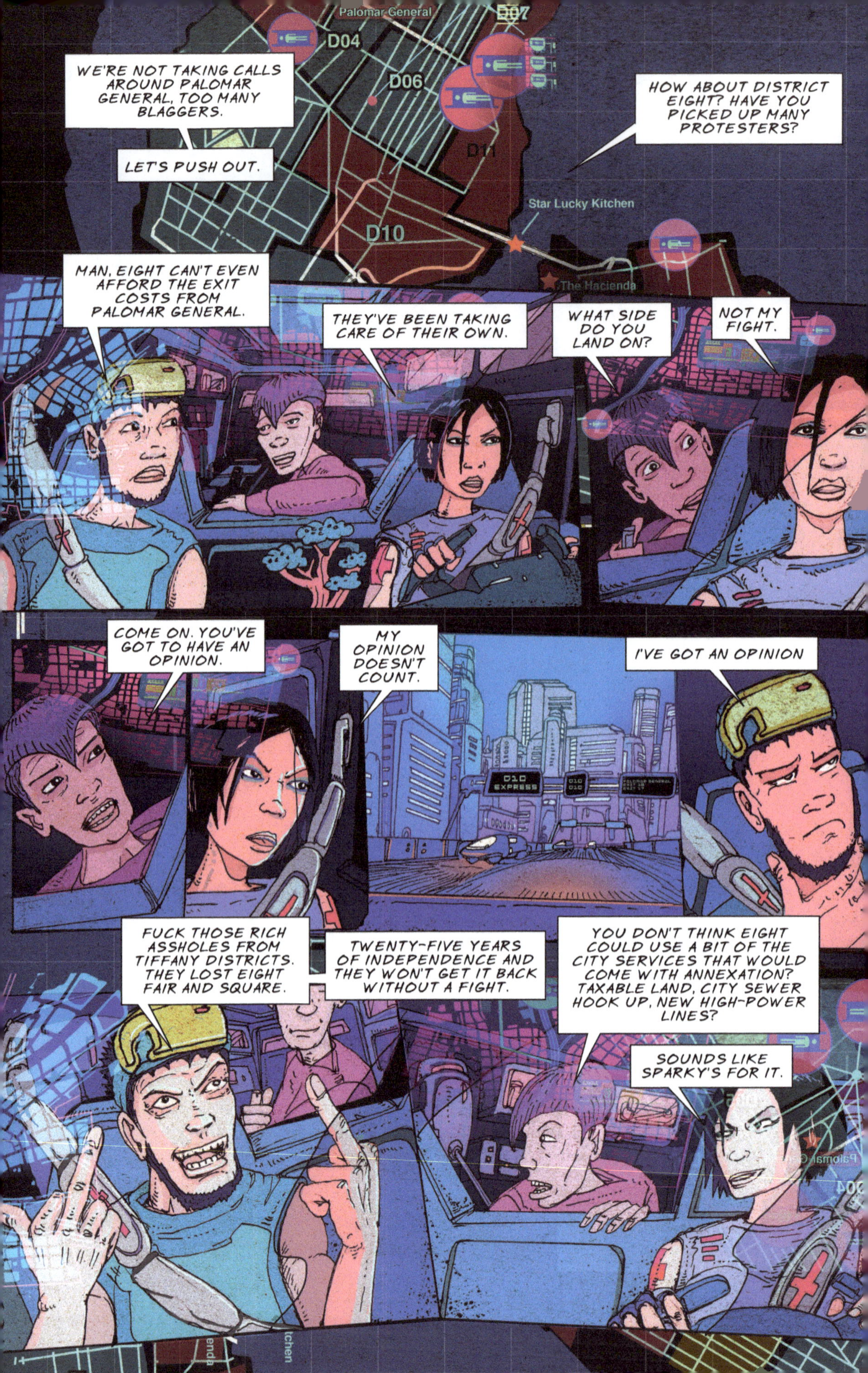

WE'RE NOT TAKING CALLS AROUND PALOMAR GENERAL, TOO MANY BLAGGERS.
LET'S PUSH OUT.
HOW ABOUT DISTRICT EIGHT? HAVE YOU PICKED UP MANY PROTESTERS?
Palomar General
D07
D04
D06
D11
D10
Star Lucky Kitchen
The Hacienda
MAN, EIGHT CAN'T EVEN AFFORD THE EXIT COSTS FROM PALOMAR GENERAL.
THEY'VE BEEN TAKING CARE OF THEIR OWN.
WHAT SIDE DO YOU LAND ON?
NOT MY FIGHT.
COME ON. YOU'VE GOT TO HAVE AN OPINION.
MY OPINION DOESN'T COUNT.
I'VE GOT AN OPINION
D10 EXPRESS
PALOMAR GENERAL
FUCK THOSE RICH ASSHOLES FROM TIFFANY DISTRICTS. THEY LOST EIGHT FAIR AND SQUARE.
TWENTY-FIVE YEARS OF INDEPENDENCE AND THEY WON'T GET IT BACK WITHOUT A FIGHT.
YOU DON'T THINK EIGHT COULD USE A BIT OF THE CITY SERVICES THAT WOULD COME WITH ANNEXATION? TAXABLE LAND, CITY SEWER HOOK UP, NEW HIGH-POWER LINES?
SOUNDS LIKE SPARKY'S FOR IT.

WAIT - NO!
I CAN SEE BOTH SIDES OF THE ISSUE. I DON'T THINK THEY'RE FRAMING THEIR ARGUMENT WELL.
THEY COULD BE GETTING A LOT FOR A LITTLE CORNER OF UNUSED LAND.
YUP. YOU'RE FOR IT.
I'M NOT FOR THE OFFER THAT'S ON THE TABLE. EIGHT SHOULDN'T TAKE IT.
WHERE ARE YOU FROM?
DISTRICT 9, BORN AND RAISED. BUT..
I LIVE IN THE LOWER EAST SIX NOW.
OOH. RICH KID HIDING OUT IN THE ROUGH NEIGHBORHOOD NEAR THE INDIE GATES.
DARING!
DISTRICT 20. BORN AND RAISED
YEAH, WHERE YOU FROM?
OK. YOU WIN. TOUGH NEIGHBORHOOD.

EVICT
YOUR
OWN

WE
LIVE

OFF

LOSE

THUMP THUMP THUMP THUMP

HEY YEAH HEY!

HEAT SEN

TIMER SET:
05:00

SCANNING
COORDINATES

WHIZZ

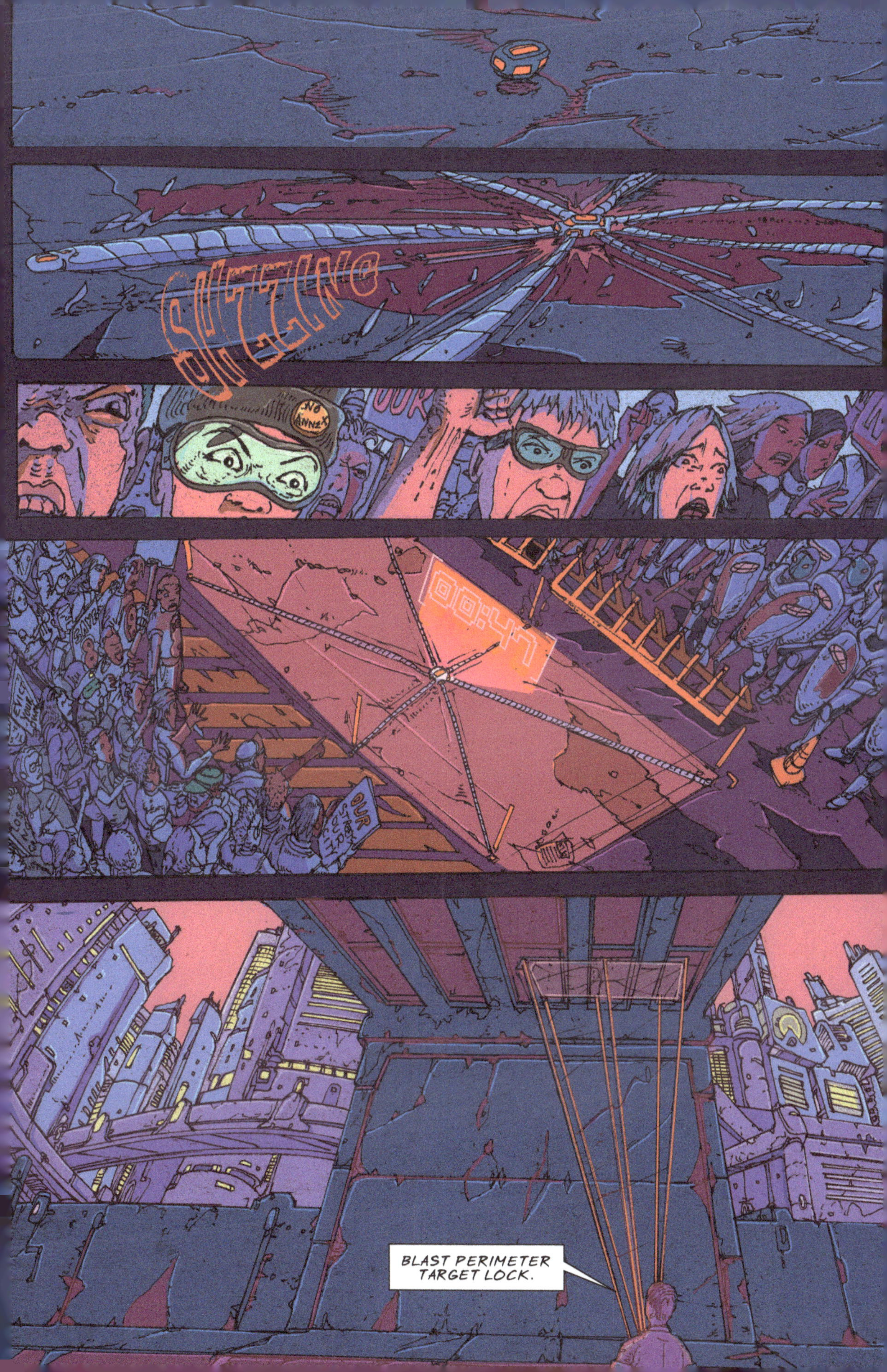

SIZZLING
NO ANNEX
OUR
00:47
BLAST PERIMETER
TARGET LOCK.

BOMB!

00:00

FRRIZZZ

AHHHHH!
FRIZZ-ZAP!
LOSE NO GROUND!
LOSE NO
BOOM!
FRIZZIZ

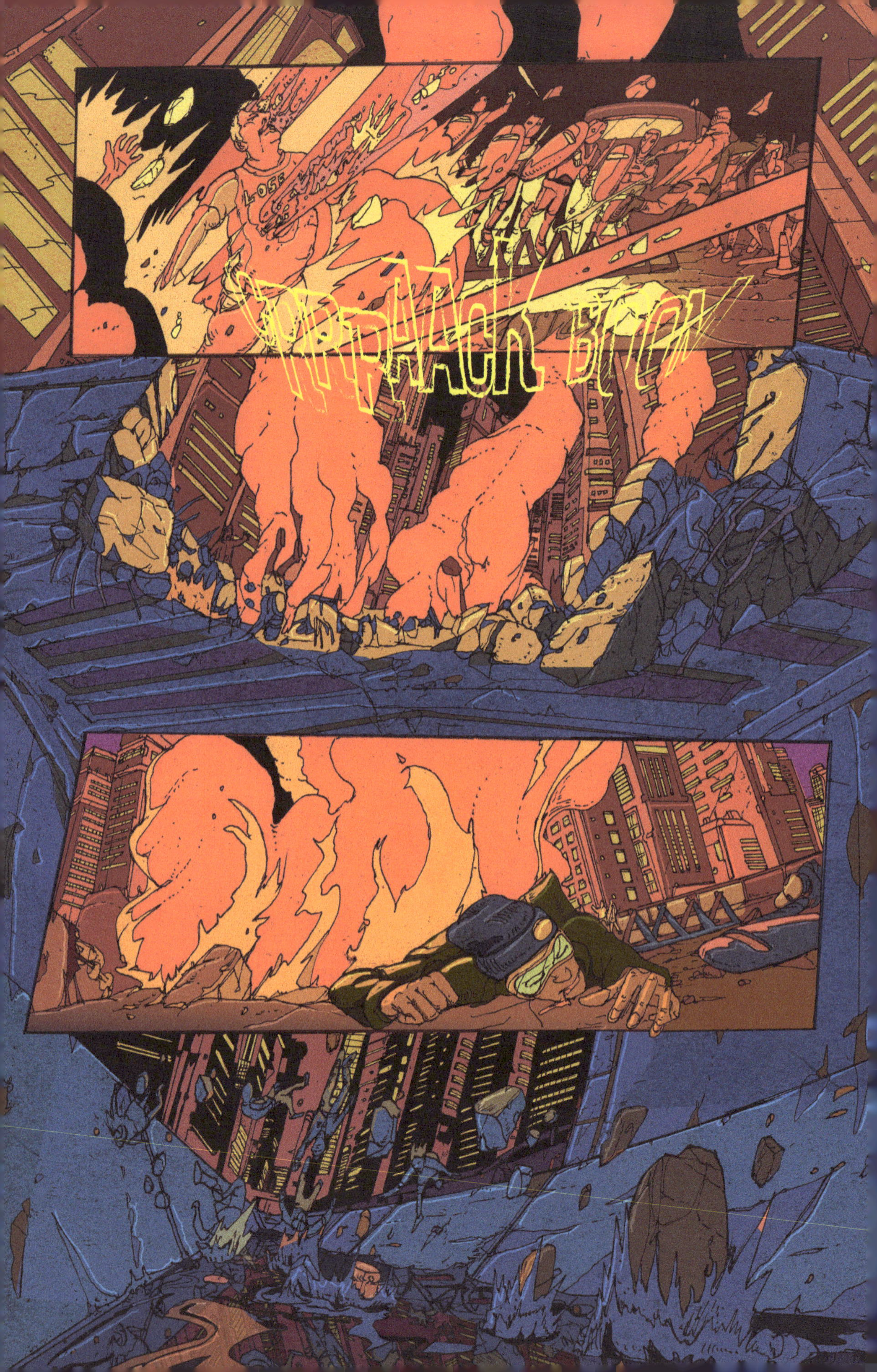
LOSER
SKAAACK BRAK

BOMB BLAST REPORTED IN DISTRICT 8. SUSPECTED TERRORIST ACTIVITY.
WE'RE HEADING THERE RIGHT??
THE BOARD'S GOING CRAZY.
ALL CITIZEN-GATES JUST CLOSED.
DAMMIT. THE STREETS ARE LOCKING UP. JUST LIKE AFTER THE STADIUM COLLAPSE IN 13 LAST YEAR.
GATECRASHERS DIDN'T GET OUT OF THAT MESS FOR 48 HOURS AND SOME ONLY GOT ONE DROP.
THIS IS MAJOR. WE NEED TO BE THERE.
NO OFFICIAL BODYCOUNT
BOMB BLAST. MANY WOUNDED
SUSPECTED TERRORIST. SUSPECTED D08 PROTESTORS
IF WE'RE GOING IN WE'VE GOT TO BE SMART ABOUT IT.
AUTHORITIES ARE ON THE SCENE

狗屁
LASER GUIDED REMOTE SHAPE CHARGE.
TARGETED FROM ABOVE - BLAST FROM BELOW.
DO NOT ENGAGE.
NOT YOUR AVERAGE PROTESTOR!
SAVE 8

BOMB SUSPECT HEADING NORTH -- ROTHMAN CANAL TOWARD DISTRICT 01 GATE.
DETECTIVE, AS LONG AS YOU'RE IN AN INDIE DISTRICT WE CAN'T HELP. CIVILIAN ACCESS ONLY.
BAM
SNAP

CRACK
911 WHAT'S YOUR EMERGENCY
NEED AN AMBULANCE. TWO INJURED. GUNSHOT WOUNDS.
S.O.R
S.O.R
141 EAST AVENUE A ADJACENT TO THE SKYWAY.
CONFIRMED. S.O.R. BUILDING DISTRICT 8.

HUH!

PALOMAR
HERE'S A DOUBLE, RIGHT ON THE EDGE OF EIGHT. WE DON'T HAVE TO CROSS THE ROTHMAN GATE.
ZERO-SEVEN SEVENTY. LOCK ON THE DROP AT 141 EAST AVENUE A - DELTA - 08.
BE ADVISED - GUNSHOT WOUNDS.
BUCKLE UP SPARKY.
D14
ACTION 77 NEWS
THE LAWLESSNESS HAS TURNED THIS ISSUE ON ITS HEAD AND AS A CITY WE CANNOT GO TO SLEEP AT NIGHT KNOWING OUR NEIGHBORS ARE CAPABLE OF SUCH VIOLENCE.
THIS IS TURNING BACK THE CLOCK THIRTY YEARS! MY HEART GOES OUT TO ALL THE INNOCENT VICTIMS OF THIS HORRIBLE AND VICIOUS ACT OF TERRORISM. OUR FOCUS NOW HAS TO BE ON SAVING AS MANY LIVES AS POSSIBLE.
DANE, WHAT IMPACT DO YOU THINK THIS WILL HAVE ON THE HEIGHTS TOWER ANNEXATION PROPOSAL?
DANE BRENNAN, CEO
CHARLOTTE, I HOPE THE CITIZENS OF DISTRICT EIGHT CAN SEE THE DRASTIC DIFFERENCE BETWEEN OUR PROPOSAL, POSITIVE URBAN RE-DEVELOPMENT AND THIS URBAN TERRORISM.
I DO SHARE MR. BRENNAN'S CONCERNS FOR THE SAFETY OF EVERY CITIZEN OF PALOMAR CITY, REGARDLESS OF WHAT DISTRICT THEY CALL HOME. BUT WE DON'T KNOW WHO'S BEHIND THIS AND WE CAN'T JUMP TO CONCLUSIONS.
52 INJURED AND COUNTING
13 DEAD
DANE BRENNAN, CEO
MAYOR GIRLE WARREN
ROTHMAN SKYWAY CLOSED FROM CITY HALL TO DISTRICT 09.

SHIT, THIS IS A S.O.R BUILDING. NOT A LOT OF GATECRASHER LOVE.
WHY DO CREEPY RELIGIOUS CULTS HAVE TO BE SO SECRETIVE?
LOCKED.
SO NOW WHAT?
GO IN THE HARD WAY OR LEAVE AND LOG A NEW DROP.
WE'RE GOING IN — I'M NOT CHASING DOWN ANOTHER DROP.
THIS IS DEFINITELY OFF THE RECORD.
DROP YOUR WEAPON.
THAT'S ON THE ROOF!
WE'RE IN!

ARCHIE, HOLD THIS!
THIS DROP SUX.

FAZZPP
AARRG GH
FAZZPP

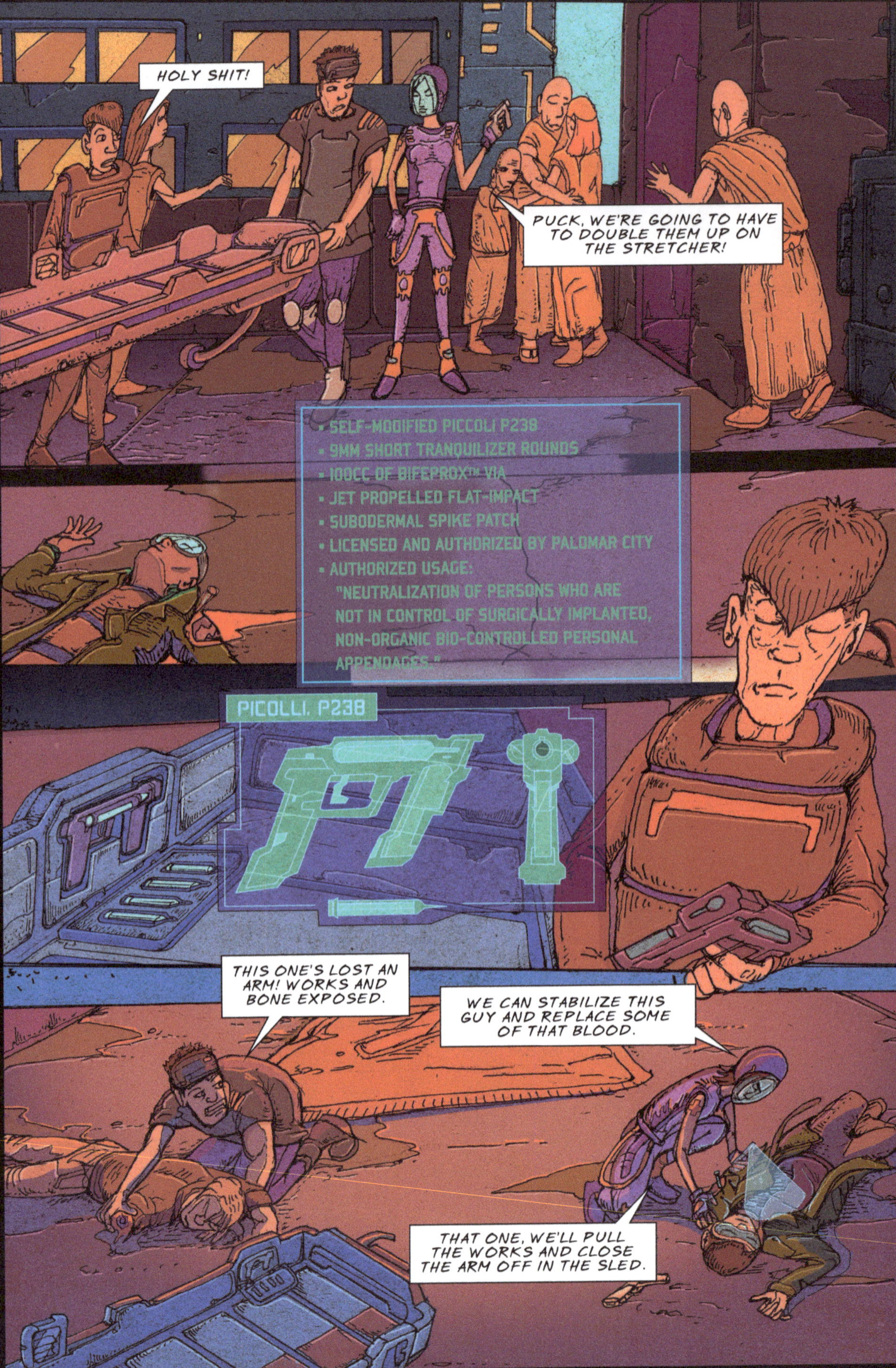

HOLY SHIT!

PUCK, WE'RE GOING TO HAVE TO DOUBLE THEM UP ON THE STRETCHER!

• SELF-MODIFIED PICCOLI P238
• 9MM SHORT TRANQUILIZER ROUNDS
• 100CC OF BIFEPROX™ VIA
• JET PROPELLED FLAT-IMPACT
• SUBODERMAL SPIKE PATCH
• LICENSED AND AUTHORIZED BY PALOMAR CITY
• AUTHORIZED USAGE:
"NEUTRALIZATION OF PERSONS WHO ARE NOT IN CONTROL OF SURGICALLY IMPLANTED, NON-ORGANIC BIO-CONTROLLED PERSONAL APPENDAGES."

PICOLLI. P238

THIS ONE'S LOST AN ARM! WORKS AND BONE EXPOSED.

WE CAN STABILIZE THIS GUY AND REPLACE SOME OF THAT BLOOD.

THAT ONE, WE'LL PULL THE WORKS AND CLOSE THE ARM OFF IN THE SLED.

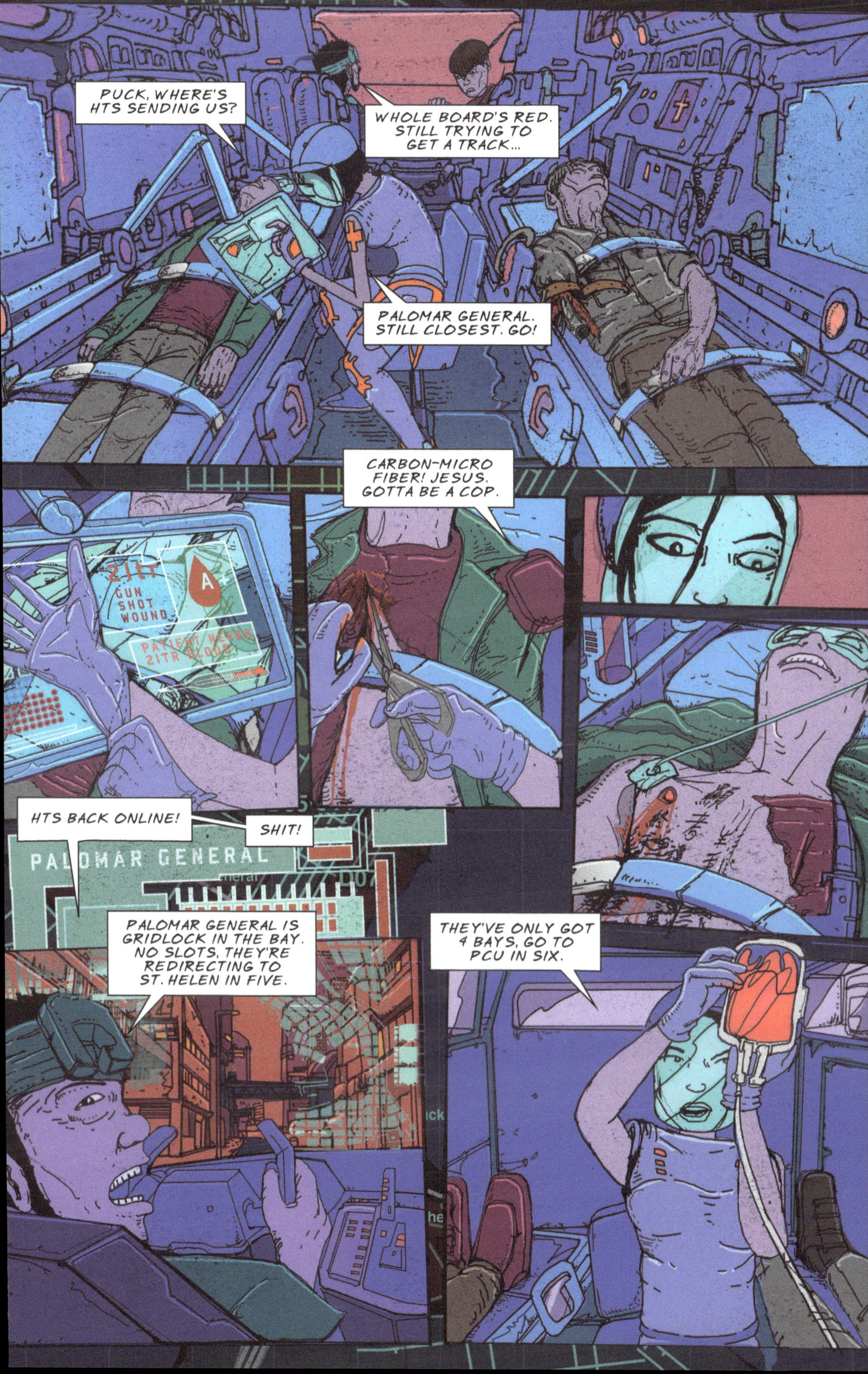

PUCK, WHERE'S HTS SENDING US?
WHOLE BOARD'S RED. STILL TRYING TO GET A TRACK...
PALOMAR GENERAL. STILL CLOSEST. GO!
CARBON-MICRO FIBER! JESUS. GOTTA BE A COP.
2LTR GUN SHOT WOUND
A+
PATIENT NEEDS 2LTR BLOOD
HTS BACK ONLINE!
SHIT!
PALOMAR GENERAL
PALOMAR GENERAL IS GRIDLOCK IN THE BAY. NO SLOTS, THEY'RE REDIRECTING TO ST. HELEN IN FIVE.
THEY'VE ONLY GOT 4 BAYS, GO TO PCU IN SIX.

14%
ALERT
PRIVATE - NO REGISTRATION
SEVERE LOWER ARM TRAUMA
TREATMENT LOG- BiteproXTM 10/1000000
SCAN RESULTS:
HONEYCOMB-TITANIUM
BONE-REPLACEMENTS
AND THIS GUY'S GOT WHITE-LABEL SUPERELECTRO WORKS? WHAT THE HELL IS GOING ON?

WE'VE GOT A SERIOUS SITUATION HERE.
YEAH, THIS ONE'S WEARING A VEST. I THINK HE'S A COP!
I THINK THAT OTHER GUY'S ONE OF THE TERRORISTS!!
CALLING: RADA
REGISTRATION
RADA, I'VE GOT A FULL HOUSE AND THEY'RE NO GOOD. ONE COULD BE STRC BUT HE'S NOT SCANNING.
THE OTHER SCANS PRIVATE BUT NO REGISTRATION — COULD BE INVOLVED WITH THE BOMBING. I HAD TO TRANQ THEM BOTH.
I DON'T HAVE THAT KIND OF TIME. NOT ENOUGH BLOOD IN THE SLED.
TAKE THEM TO CITY OF MERCY IN D-TWO.
THEN THEY'RE GONNA HAVE TO RUN THIN. BETTER THAN GETTING TURNED AWAY AT PCU. GET THEM THERE AS FAST AS YOU CAN. DROP EM' AND GO.
REPORTER STILL WITH YOU?
I DIDN'T KNOW THAT WAS OPTIONAL.
STILL HERE! GETTING A GREAT STORY.

HE DIDN'T MAKE THE MEET.
DAMMIT!
INTERMITTENT TRACKING. HE TRAVELED 200 YARDS AFTER THE BLAST AND STOPPED. NOTHING SINCE THEN.
HIS RECORD IS CLEAN. HIS SCAN IS CLEAN. ALL HIS WORKS ARE WHITE-LABEL SUPERELECTRO.
HIS TERMINATION CLAUSE IS FULL-ZERO CORRECT?
YES, BUT WE CAN ONLY INITIATE IF HE COMES BACK ON-LINE. I'M GOING TO START WITH REVIVE. THE TWINJECT SIGNAL IS PULSE-RADIO. STILL NO GUARANTEES IF HE'S OUT OF RANGE.
IF HE'S CONSCIOUS IT'LL PUT HIM IN IMMEDIATE SHOCK.
WORKS EITHER WAY.

HEY BILL, LOOKS LIKE OUR CAMPERS LOST A BIT OF FIGHT AFTER THEY BLEW THEMSELVES UP.
ALL DUE RESPECT MR. BRENNAN BUT IT LOOKS LIKE IT WAS JUST THE WORK OF A SMALL SPLINTER GROUP OF ANARCHISTS.
PALOMAR POLICE
PALOMAR POLICE
I DON'T THINK SO BILL. A PLAN LIKE THIS GOES ALL THE WAY UP TO THE COMMITTEE.
ARE WE ON THE SAME PAGE?
PALOMAR POLICE
ASSHOLE.

YOU SHOT ME!
I'M STRC.
YOU WERE A DANGER TO ME AND THE PUBLIC.
YOU DIDN'T IDENTIFY YOURSELF.
OWWW!!
狗屁
WENT STRAIGHT THROUGH. NO MAJOR DAMAGE.
STOP THIS SLED RIGHT NOW. CALL IN BACK UP.
WE'RE NOT STOPPING UNTIL THE HOSPITAL.
I BARELY HAVE ENOUGH BLOOD TO KEEP YOU BOTH ALIVE UNTIL WE GET THERE!
SUBJECT: ANONYMOUS-029
PROTOCOL: TWINJECT SUBDERMAL RADIOPULSE
ACTION: EXECUTE POSITIVE RESPONSE.
A+

UNNRG GH!
THREE MINUTES TO CITY D2 GATE.
HOLY SHIT!
OUOFF!
SPLAMASH
CLUCHUNK

SKRAANG
GRRIND
DANGER
DISPOSAL
DANGEROUS
GOODS
HELLP!

AARRGGH
NNUNCH!
SPLiiNGE
JAM!

SKREERAP
PUCK, NOTIFY DISPATCH WE LOST A STRETCHER ON COLUMBIA STREET.
STOP THIS AMBULANCE NOW!
SIGNAL CITY OF MERCY. WE'RE OUT OF BLOOD. USING MY LAST HEMO-JECT.

CITY OF MERCY HOSPITAL
I SAVED THE GOOD GUY'S LIFE.
OK.
YOU DON'T STRIKE ME AS MILITARY. WHERE'D THOSE MOVES COME FROM?
YOU LET THE BAD GUY GO!
THEY LOOKED LIKE DISTRICT 11 SPEED-FIGHTS. YOU GROW UP IN STACY HOUSES?
INTAKE! GOTTA GUNSHOT WOUND - STABLE.
WHERE YOU THINK YOU'RE GOING?
AND YOU PULLED HIS WETWORK SO FAST I'D THINK YOU WERE GOING TO SELL IT FOR TECH?
YOUR SLED IS A CRIME SCENE.
07-70
PARAMEDIC ID:
HIXON SPENCER
YOU CAN'T...

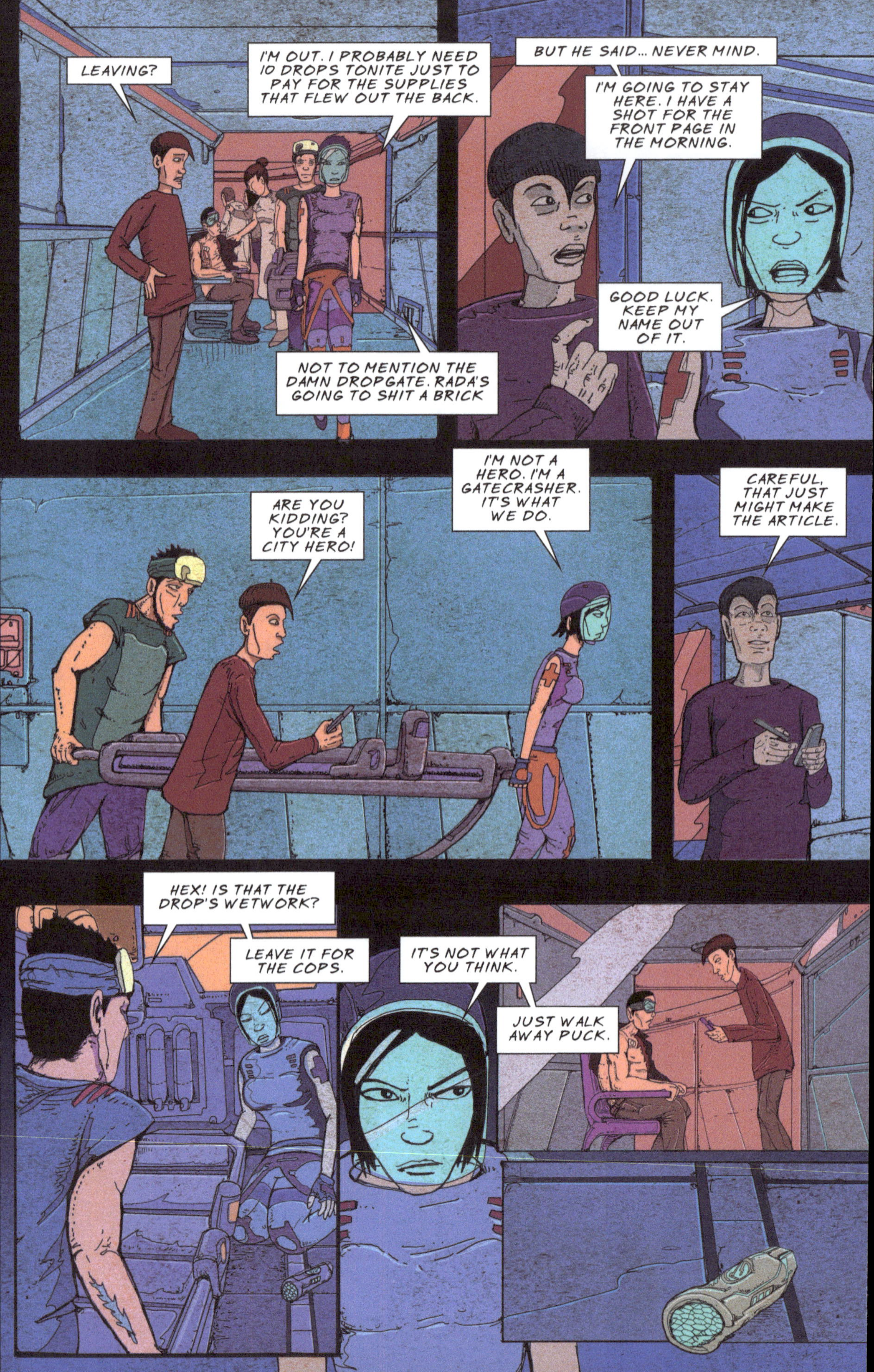

LEAVING?
I'M OUT. I PROBABLY NEED 10 DROPS TONITE JUST TO PAY FOR THE SUPPLIES THAT FLEW OUT THE BACK.
NOT TO MENTION THE DAMN DROPGATE. RADA'S GOING TO SHIT A BRICK
BUT HE SAID... NEVER MIND.
I'M GOING TO STAY HERE. I HAVE A SHOT FOR THE FRONT PAGE IN THE MORNING.
GOOD LUCK. KEEP MY NAME OUT OF IT.
ARE YOU KIDDING? YOU'RE A CITY HERO!
I'M NOT A HERO. I'M A GATECRASHER. IT'S WHAT WE DO.
CAREFUL, THAT JUST MIGHT MAKE THE ARTICLE.
HEX! IS THAT THE DROP'S WETWORK?
LEAVE IT FOR THE COPS.
IT'S NOT WHAT YOU THINK.
JUST WALK AWAY PUCK.

GATECRASHER
DAILY LOG

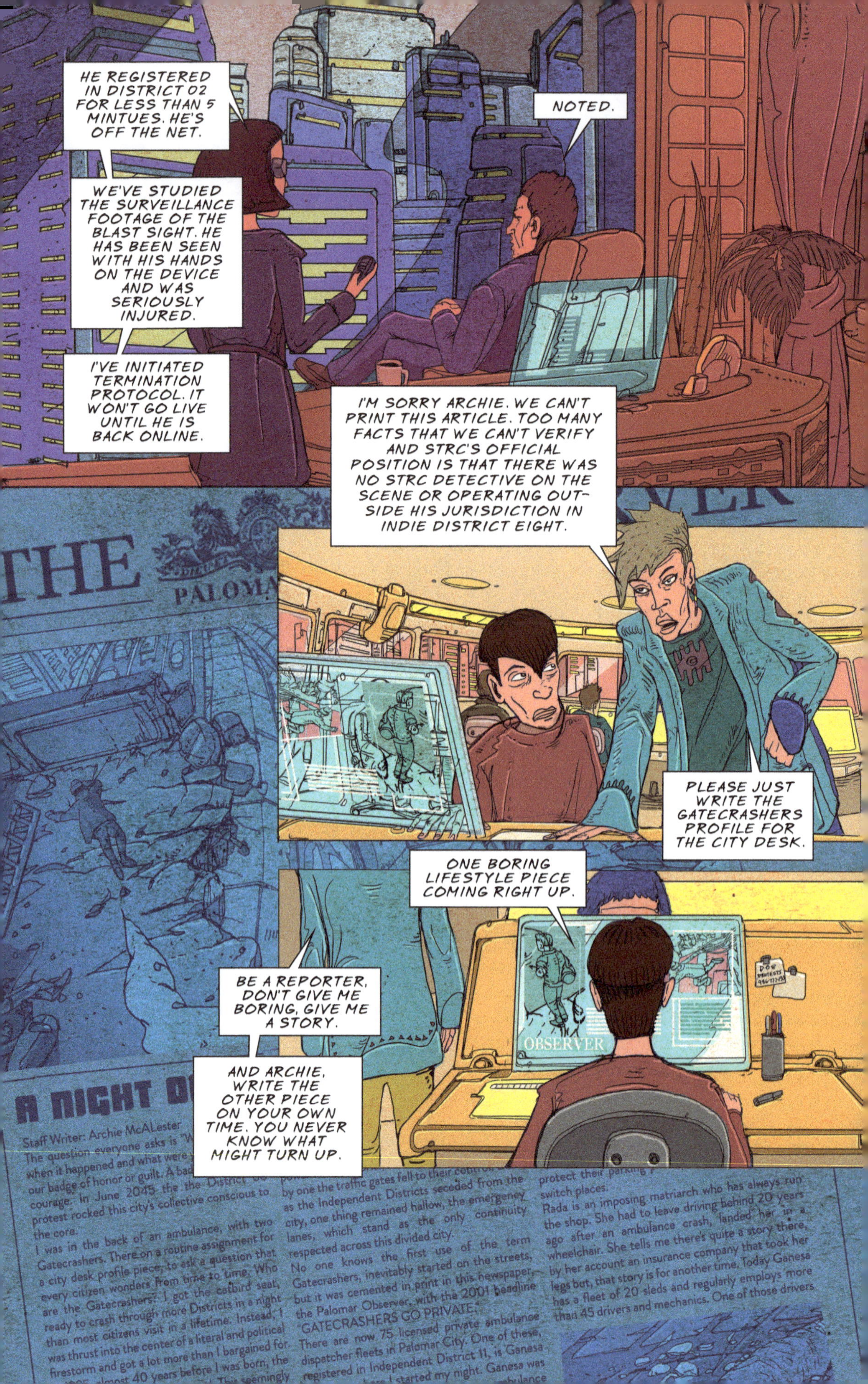

HE REGISTERED IN DISTRICT 02 FOR LESS THAN 5 MINTUES. HE'S OFF THE NET.
NOTED.
WE'VE STUDIED THE SURVEILLANCE FOOTAGE OF THE BLAST SIGHT. HE HAS BEEN SEEN WITH HIS HANDS ON THE DEVICE AND WAS SERIOUSLY INJURED.
I'VE INITIATED TERMINATION PROTOCOL. IT WON'T GO LIVE UNTIL HE IS BACK ONLINE.
I'M SORRY ARCHIE. WE CAN'T PRINT THIS ARTICLE. TOO MANY FACTS THAT WE CAN'T VERIFY AND STRC'S OFFICIAL POSITION IS THAT THERE WAS NO STRC DETECTIVE ON THE SCENE OR OPERATING OUT- SIDE HIS JURISDICTION IN INDIE DISTRICT EIGHT.
PLEASE JUST WRITE THE GATECRASHERS PROFILE FOR THE CITY DESK.
ONE BORING LIFESTYLE PIECE COMING RIGHT UP.
BE A REPORTER, DON'T GIVE ME BORING, GIVE ME A STORY.
AND ARCHIE, WRITE THE OTHER PIECE ON YOUR OWN TIME. YOU NEVER KNOW WHAT MIGHT TURN UP.
THE PALOMAR OBSERVER
A NIGHT OU
OBSERVER
Staff Writer: Archie McALester
The question everyone asks is "W
when it happened and what were
our badge of honor or guilt. A ba
courage. In June 2045 the the District
protest rocked this city's collective conscious to
the core.
I was in the back of an ambulance, with two
Gatecrashers. There on a routine assignment for
a city desk profile piece, to ask a question that
every citizen wonders from time to time. Who
are the Gatecrashers? I got the catbird seat,
ready to crash through more Districts in a night
than most citizens visit in a lifetime. Instead, I
was thrust into the center of a literal and political
firestorm and got a lot more than I bargained for.
almost 40 years before I was born, the
seemingly
by one the traffic gates fell to their con
as the Independent Districts seceded
city, one thing remained hallow, the e
lanes, which stand as the only continuity
respected across this divided city.
No one knows the first use of the term
Gatecrashers, inevitably started on t
but it was cemented in print in this newspaper,
the Palomar Observer, with the 2001 deadline
"GATECRASHERS GO PRIVATE."
There are now 75 licensed private ambulance
dispatcher fleets in Palomar City. One of these,
registered in Independent District 11, is Ganesa
Ganesa was
I started my night. Ganesa
ambulance
protect their parking ?
switch places.
Rada is an imposing matriarch who has always run
the shop. She had to leave driving behind 20 years
ago after an ambulance crash, landed her in a
wheelchair. She tells me there's quite a story there,
by her account an insurance company that took her
legs but, that story is for another time. Today Ganesa
has a fleet of 20 sleds and regularly employs more
than 45 drivers and mechanics. One of those drivers

ne Brennan and his camp would simplify
nexation of D08 corner to be about land
xes. They live in such a myopic world
ivilege that they can't see the soft impa[ct]
development. For the people of District
any of whom will have no noticeable gain from
he added tax revenue and concessions that the
developers and city are offering, this displace-
ment goes much further. Not just the displace-
ment of six square blocks the super-luxury
complex will occupy, but the eventual creep of
the myriad of services and stores that fan out
around it to support the lifestyle of the new
residents and the inevitable gentrification and
housing that will emerge. The current citizens of
this neighborhood will be priced out of the new
housing, shopping and business that the D08
Corner will bring. The bodegas and kiosks will be
replaced by PIM-free foodstuffs, real perishable
meat and vegetables, and lifestyle stores so far
beyond the reach of the average citizen that we
will be re-kindling the ire that led to the
secession in the first place. For the D08
Committee I'd ask, why hasn't there been a
realistic counter-offer? One that could actually
go to bettering the District as a whole? Where
are the demands for infrastructure additions?
Extend a sewer line all the way from the D08
corner to the norther District 09 gate.
Reposition net towers for actual coverage
throughout District 08. Are the only demands
on the table going straight to Committee
? These are the questions that brought
protest

GOD DAMMIT MELITA.
I CAN'T PICK
YOU UP TODAY.

HOW ARE YOU GOING
TO GET HOME?

RECIPIENT: SHMULEK
DATA PK SND.
//:ENCRYPTION 457C
3fa9f2a6o4c2b440fb6f676076

GONE TO D. 04
BACK BY NOON

MELITA
BABY
TOYS

ALARM SET: 17:00

HEY SHMULEK. IT'S HEX.

YEAH, IT'S BEEN AGES.

DO YOU HAVE
TIME TO LOOK AT
SOMETHING
FOR ME?

DRAFT REV2
A. MCALESTER

METRO SECTION | CITY JOBS

A NIGHT OF GATECRASHING
by Archie McAlester

Last night, Palomar City experienced the single worst episode of violence since the Culture Clashes of the last century as an explosion on the Rothman Skyway killed dozens of citizens and injured hundreds more who had gathered to protest the annexation and commercial development of a small corner of District 8 by the industrial titan, Dane Brennan.

Brennan has said that in the aftermath of this tragic loss of life "our focus now, more than ever, should be on saving lives by letting Palomar evolve the way all cities do. Through structured economic development, Palomar will be able to assure a better life for everyone, including the citizens of District 8."

Brennan has overlooked one key fact of his argument. It's exactly this type of typopolitics that got us into the mess we have today. A mess that is built on the back of poorly designed city improvements, the Gates themselves.

During last night's attack, I was in the back of an ambulance for what was supposed to be a simple ride-along with an emergency medical crew, the type of crew that has free run of the city – the unofficial privilege of being a Gatecrasher – after which I would write an innocuous column about these everyday heroes. When the call came in, we drove through an already tense city that was suddenly thrust into fear, confusion, and terror.

As we approached the scene, I realized that Palomar's current social problems and the Gatecrashers were inextricably linked – and that they may also lead to our salvation.

DRAFT REV2
A. MCALESTER

METRO SECTION | CITY JOBS

"A NIGHT OF GATECRASHING" *CONTINUED FROM PAGE 65*

CONTINUED FROM PAGE 65

The Gatecrashers began as quick-fix solution to another fumbled urban initiative — the Traffic Gate System. Designed to curb congestion, this convoluted series of barriers, gates, and portals would have also, in theory, refilled city coffers as citizens and businesses were charged tolls for passage between city neighborhoods. This defined the Districts we know today.

The Gates, however, had the opposite effect as near total gridlock strangled traffic and the Districts. With little to no crossover between their residents, Districts became socio-ethnic ghettos. It was only later, after incidents of violence along gate lines began to rise, that City Hall realized they had carved Palomar up into a series of pressure cookers of discontent where access to city services became directly related to one's affluence.

As the social divisions within grew more dramatic, the administration came up with a plan for an urban emergency medical service that could pass through gates at will in special-use lanes. The public loved the idea as it promised, at long last, equal access to medical care no matter where you lived. They also quickly came up with a nickname for this new EMS corps — The Gatecrashers.

The Gatecrashers' mission, which began simply as the treatment or transport of the sick or injured, was also one of good will and one of the last hopes of a city that was becoming more divided and buried under the increasingly contradictory spin from both City Hall and District leaders alike. Simply look back at old photos to see the shiny new ambulances manned by clean cut EMTs who embodied hope for the future.

Now, nearly three generations later, Palomar's identity as a single community is all but forgotten. The Gatecrashers who were once the symbol of a re-integrated city, are being steadily undermined by rumors of malpractice and trafficking in stolen wetwork and body parts even as they represent a bygone era, when we were all citizens of the same community and not opponents on the battlefield of urbanization.

I would love to share with you the details of my experience in the back of the sled last night, but the events of the evening have been classified as a threat to public safety and city security. I don't know how I'll get the information out but I will find a way.

What I can tell you is that I was hopeful to see that selfless hard work in the proudest tradition of the Gatecrashers still goes on. When I asked my guide for the night (who doesn't want her name used) why she was a Gatecrasher, her reply was as simple as it was stunning.

"This town just needs someone to take care of it. I guess that's me."

The Gatecrashers will return in Book Two.

A NIGHT OF GATECRASHING
BOOK ONE

PALOMAR CITY POLICE
INTELLIGENCE BUREAU
DISTRICT PROFILES

STRC HISTORY

FORMED IN 1980 CONCURRENTLY WITH THE PASSING OF THE TRAFFIC GATE SYSTEM, TRAFFIC RESPONSE CONTROL UNIT (TRCU), A BRANCH OF THE PALOMAR CITY POLICE DEPARTMENT (PCPD) WAS FOCUSED ON OPERATIONS FOR THE NEW TRAFFIC CONTROL SYSTEM. AT FIRST THE TRCU OFFICERS RESEMBLED PORT AUTHORITY POLICE, TASKED WITH KEEPING THE PEACE AND ENFORCING TRAFFIC COMPLIANCE AT THE GATES. AT THE DAWN OF THE CULTURE CLASHES IN 2003 AND WITH THE ERECTION OF THE DISTRICT 05 WALL, THE DEPARTMENT WAS RENAMED SECURITY TRAFFIC RESPONSE CONTROL FORCE OR STRC. PATROLMEN WERE RE-CHRISTENED THE 'STRIKE FORCE' AND BECAME A SWAT-LIKE SPECIAL FORCES DIVISION OF THE PCPD.

THE STREET NAME FOR THIS DEPARTMENT COMES FROM ITS ACRONYM STRC - "STRIKE".

KIDNAPPING & RANSOM

DURING THE CULTURE CLASHES THE CITY SAW DOUBLE DIGIT INCREASES IN KIDNAPPINGS AND RANSOM (K&R) CASES. A SPECIAL K&R DEPARTMENT IN STRC WAS CREATED, KR:STRC. THIS ELITE UNIT WAS DOWNSIZED IN 2028 AFTER 4 STRAIGHT YEARS OF DECLINING CALLS, BUT THE LEGEND OF THE DEPARTMENT STILL LIVES STRONG. THE KR DEPARTMENT'S NICKNAME WITHIN STRC WAS KILL & RETRIEVE, ALLUDING TO THEIR SUCCESS RATE ON RETURNING WITH LIVING HOS-TAGES. BUT TO THIS DAY, K&R TEAMS HAVE A REPUTATION OF BEING THE TOUGHEST, BRIGHTEST AND THE BEST OF THE BEST.

DISTRICT 05

THE ORIGINAL TIFFANY DISTRICT. THE NEIGHBORHOOD IS HOME TO PALOMAR'S WEALTHY AND ELITE, POPULATED BY BANKERS, POLITICIANS AND UPPER-CRUST CELEBRITIES. DISTRICT 05 WAS THE GATES CATALYST, BORN OUT OF THE ENCROACHING INDUSTRIAL DISTRICTS WHICH WERE EVOLVING INTO MORE SHANTY-TOWN LIKE COMMUNITIES OF LABORERS AS SKYNESTING AND HUTMENTS BECAME MORE POPULAR. THE AFFLUENT RESIDENTS HIRED PRIVATE SECURITY TO PATROL THE GATES IN RESPONSE TO THE 'LOW DISTRICTS' OVERPOWERING THE CITY AND TAKING CONTROL OF THE GATES FOR NEFARIOUS PURPOSES. OVER TIME THE STRC FORCE MADE DISTRICT 05 THEIR HOME BASE AND HQ. THE GATES IN AND OUT OF DISTRICT 05 ARE THE MOST HEAVILY FORTIFIED AND UNLIKE SOME OF THE OUTLYING ABANDONED GATES, ARE MANNED BY ARMED STRC PATROLS 24 HOURS A DAY.

STRC.WATCH

- DANE BRENNAN   [LINK]
- MAYOR GIRLIE WARREN   [LINK]
- HON. CORNBLUTH   [LINK]

STRC.STAT

POP CENSUS	48,765
POP EST.	42,000
STRC CMD	FT. CENTURY
PCFD CMD	LADDER 21
	ENGINE 13
BORD E.	BROADWAY
BORD W.	CIVIC PLAZA
BORD N.	ROTHMAN BLVD
BORD S.	THE MILE
BODYMOD	AGELESS
	BROADCASTERS

DISTRICT 09

IN THE EARLY 1900'S PALOMAR CITY WAS A MAJOR INTERNATIONAL SHIPPING PORT. THE WATER-WAYS WERE LINED WITH DOCKS AND THERE WAS A RAILWAY SYSTEM TO SUPPORT THEM. AS THE CITY AND COUNTRY CHANGED OVER THE COURSE OF THE CENTURY, THE SHIPPING INDUSTRY STREAMLINED AND CONSOLIDATED. IN PALOMAR CITY THE MAJORITY OF THE DOCKS FELL OUT OF SERVICE AND WHETHER THROUGH NATURAL OR UNNATURAL SELECTION, THE DOCKS OF DISTRICT 09 REMAIN THE ONLY FUNCTIONING OPERATION IN TOWN. THESE DOCKS AND ALL THE CARGO THAT COMES AND GOES THROUGH THEM ARE CONTROLLED BY THE INDUSTRIAL BEHEMOTH, BRENNAN/STEINER, INC, RUN BY FIFTH GENERATION OLIGARCH, DANE BRENNAN.

THE OFFICIAL PORT AUTHORITY OF PALOMAR CITY OPERATES OUT OF DISTRICT 09.

STRC.WATCH

* DANE BRENNAN   [LINK]
* MAYOR GIRLIE WARREN   [LINK]

STRC.STAT

POP CENSUS	48,765
POP EST.	42,000
STRC CMD	FT. CENTURY
PCFD CMD	LADDER 21
	ENGINE 13
BORD E.	CITY RIVER
BORD W.	CIVIC PLAZA
BORD N.	ROTHMAN BLVD
BORD S.	THE MILE
BODYMOD	AGELESS
	BROADCASTERS

DISTRICT 10

DISTRICT 10 WAS A MAJOR INDUSTRIAL AND FACTORY SECTION OF PALOMAR CITY. MANY OF TODAY'S CONCERNS WITH SKY-NESTING AND IMMIGRATION WERE BORN IN DISTRICT 10. THE MAJORITY OF THE POPULATION IN DISTRICT 10 IS FROM SOUTH EAST ASIA. IN THE 1990'S DUE TO POLITICAL SHIFTS IN THEIR HOME-LANDS, HUNDREDS OF THOUSANDS OF IMMIGRANTS SET OUT FOR AMERICA. TENS OF THOUSANDS LANDED ILLEGALLY AT THE PORTS OF DISTRICT 09 WHICH MARKED THE GREAT POPULATION BOOM. THESE IMMIGRANT WORKERS WERE THEN FUNNELED ON FOOT, IN CONTAINERS OR IN TRUCKS AND TRANSPORT TRAINS, THROUGH A SE-RIES OF INTERCONNECTED FACTORIES AND WAREHOUSES, INTO DISTRICT 10.

BECAUSE THE GATES HAD ESSENTIAL-LY CREATED A WALLED-OFF GHETTO OF CULTURAL AND ETHNIC CONCENTRATION, THE FLOOD OF IMMIGRANTS INTO DISTRICT 10 COULD NOT EASILY TRAVEL THROUGH-OUT THE CITY, WHICH THEREFORE HINDERED ANY ASSIMILATION. AS THE POPULATION OF THE DISTRICT SWELLED IN THE MID 90'S, FACTORY OWNERS AND LANDLORDS FACED WITH BEING UNABLE TO EXPAND HOUSING LATERALLY, BEGAN TO BUILD VERTICAL-LY. THE NEW CONSTRUCTION ON TOP OF EXISTING BUILDINGS CREATED DORMITO-RIES, OR EVEN FULL, THRIVING, CITY-LIKE COMMUNITIES OF IMMIGRANT FAMILIES HIGH ABOVE STREET-LEVEL. THIS BECAME KNOWN AS SKYNESTING.

AFTER HUNDREDS WERE KILLED IN A FEW DEVASTATING FIRES, THE CITY GOT THEIR FIRST GLIMPSE BEHIND THE DOORS OF THESE "SHANTY-TOWNS IN THE SKY". THE DEMANDS FOR OVERSIGHT WERE RAISED AND SO WAS AN ARMY OF OPPOSITION, NOT JUST FROM FACTORY OWNERS, BUT FROM THE IMMIGRANTS THEMSELVES. THE THREAT OF REGULATION PUT FEAR AND CONTEMPT IN THE HEARTS AND MINDS OF THESE SEEMINGLY JUXTAPOSED GROUPS AND A DANGEROUS SYMBIOSIS WAS FORMED.

IN 2000 THE CULTURE CLASHES BEGAN IN THE HEART OF DISTRICT 10, WHEN A FIF-TY-STRONG STRC FORCE UNSUCCESSFULLY STORMED THE YANGON BUILDING. AT THE END OF THE DAY, BETWEEN BOTH SIDES, 15 WERE DEAD AND FOR THE NEXT 10 YEARS THE DISTRICT FOUGHT TO GAIN CONTROL OF THEIR OWN BORDER AND GATES. THE ULTIMATE RESULT WAS THAT MORE POWER WAS SHIFTED TO THE LOCAL LEADERS TO GOVERN THEIR OWN DISTRICTS, INCLUDING CONTROL OF THE GATES THEMSELVES.

STRC.STAT

POP CENSUS	115,765
POP EST.	142,000
STRC CMD	FT. TANGLEWOOD
PCFD CMD	LADDER 18 ENGINE 09
BODYMOD	

STRC.STAT

- ESTEFAN HAWK   〖LINK〗
- BILL STACY DEC.   〖LINK〗
- HIXON "HEX" SPENCER

STRC.STAT

POP CENSUS	48,765
POP EST.	42,000
STRC CMD	FT. FIRELIGHT
PCFD CMD	LADDER 10
	ENGINE 04
BORDERS	
BODYMOD	SKINS
	〖reptilian〗

DISTRICT 11

DISTRICT 11 IS THE HOME OF THE VERY FIRST WETWORK CALLED SKINS, INVENTED BY THE NOW REIGNING CRIME LORD, ESTEFAN HAWK.

DISTRICT 11 CEMENTED ITS POSITION IN THE TOP RANKS OF THE GRAY MARKET ECONOMY DURING THE CULTURE CLASHES AS A PRIMARY CONDUIT OF SUPPLIES, FOOD AND WEAPONS TO DISTRICT 10 AND OTHERS. FORTUNES WERE MADE AND THE SEATS OF POWER WERE ESTABLISHED. THE PRIMARY FORCE OF INDUSTRY IN DISTRICT 11 IS WET-WARE: ILLEGAL WETWORK TISSUE, PARTS AND SUPPLIES. THESE ARE TRADED THROUGHOUT THE CITY AND EXPORTED TO OTHER COUNTRIES AS WELL.

STRC.STAT

- ESTEFAN HAWK   〖LINK〗
- BILL STACY DEC. 〖LINK〗
- HIXON "HEX" SPENCER

STRC.STAT

POP CENSUS	48,765
POP EST.	42,000
STRC CMD	FT. FIRELIGHT
PCFD CMD	LADDER 10
	ENGINE 04
BORDERS	
BODYMOD	SKINS
	〖reptilian〗

DISTRICT 20

DISTRICT 20 IS ON THE SOUTHEAST SIDE OF CITY RIVER, CONNECTED TO THE MAIN CITY BY THE EAST SIDE BRIDGE. DISTRICT 20 IS ALSO KNOWN AS THE HACIENDA, REFERENCING THE CITY HOUSING PROJECT, HACIENDA HOUSES, WHICH WERE TAKEN OVER BY RESIDENTS DURING THE CULTURE CLASHES. DISTRICT 20 HAS BEEN KNOWN TO UTILIZE THE LONG-ABANDONED DOCKS ON CITY RIVER TO IMPORT AND EXPORT A SMALL NATION'S WORTH OF BLACK MARKET GOODS. IN RECENT MONTHS AN ILLEGAL CONSTRUCTION PROJECT HAS BEGUN ON THE DOCKS. THIS HAS CAUGHT THE ATTENTION OF CITY COUNCIL AND MAYOR WARREN. BUT NO CITY LAWS HAVE BEEN ENFORCED IN DISTRICT 20 SINCE IT WAS EMANCIPATED IN THE CITYWIDE DISTRICT SECESSIONS OF 2028.

DISTRICT 08

THROUGHOUT THE HISTORY OF PALOMAR CITY, DISTRICT 08 HAS AS ALWAYS BEEN AN ECONOMICALLY DEPRESSED AND FORGOTTEN ZONE, AN ACTUAL LOWLANDS IN THE SHADOW OF THE CAPITAL, DOWN THE HILL FROM IT'S RICH NEIGHBORS INDISTRICTS 05 AND 09. DISTRICT 08'S PORTS LOST FAVOR IN THE LATE 1920S AS DISTRICT 09'S INDUSTRIAL INFLU-ENCE SKYROCKETED. THE GREAT CONSTRUCTION BOOM OF SKYSCRAPERS IN THE 50'S AND 60'S PASSED IT BY. IT'S SKYLINE IS LOW, TURN-OF-THE-CENTURY BUILDINGS SURROUNDED BY LAYER UPON LAYER OF SPRAWL-ING SQUATTER CITIES, WHICH CLIMB PRECAIOUSLY HIGHER INTO THE AIR EVERY DAY ON UNSTABLE, MAKESHIFT FOUNDATIONS.

THE ROTHMAN SKYWAY HAS NO EXITS IN DISTRICT 08. DURING THE CULTURE CLASHES OF THE 90'S THE REFUGEES FROM OTHER DISTRICTS FLOCKED TO THE MARSHLANDS AROUND THE DISUSED WATERFRONT AND SHANTY TOWNS WERE BORN. DISTRICT 08'S INDEPENDENCE WAS BORN NOT OF ACTIVISM, BUT BY CITY HALL'S OBJECTION TO BUILDING AND SUPPORTING INFRASTRUCTURE FOR IT'S DISAFFECTED MASSES. UN-LIKE THE DICTATORIAL DISTRICT LEADERS OF THE OTHER INDEPENDENT DISTRICTS, DISTRICT 08'S POVERTY BECAME IT'S RALLYING POINT, A COMMON HARDSHIP, AND FROM THIS IT'S GOVERNING COMMITTEE WAS BORN. THE D08 COMMITTEE IS CONSTANTLY AT ODDS WITH ITS SPIRIT AND IDENTITY OF INDEPENDENCE AND ITS DESIRE TO RE-JOIN THE CITY FOR SERVICES AND INFRASTRUCTURE.

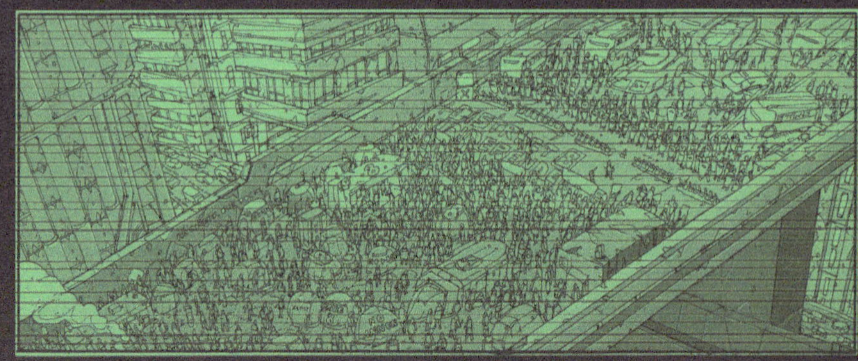

RIVERTOWN

UNOFFICIALLY KNOWN AS DISTRICT 99, RIVERTOWN IS ON THE EDGE OF THE CITY JUST PAST THE PORTS ON THE CITY SOUND. IN 2027 THE CONTAINER SHIP, PING VENTURE, RAN-AGROUND EN ROUTE TO DISTRICT 10. WHEN SUPPORT CREWS ARRIVED THEY FOUND OVER 300 ILLEGAL IMMIGRANTS IN THE CONVERTED CONTAINERS. PALOMAR CITY OFFICIALS DENIED IMMUNITY TO THE IMMIGRANTS AND THREATENED TO TOW THE SHIP BACK INTO THE OCEAN. IN A CITY STILL DIVIDED OVER THE SIEGE OF DISTRICT 10 A MERE TWO YEARS EARLIER, THE PING VENTURE BECAME ANOTHER HIGH PROFILE SLAP IN THE FACE TO THE CITY COUNCIL, WHICH STARTED A STANDOFF BETWEEN THE IMMIGRANTS ON THE SHIP, THEIR SUPPORTERS, AND THE CITY. THREE MONTHS INTO THE STAND-OFF TWO CONTAINERSHIPS MADE A DARING ATTEMPT TO BRING SUPPLIES, BUT BOTH RAN-AGROUND. THE CITY COUNCIL BACKED DOWN FROM ITS ORIGINAL DEMANDS AND SOUGHT A COMPRISE. MEANWHILE THE THREE CONTAINER SHIPS WERE WELDED SIDE BY SIDE BY THOSE LIVING AT THE EDGE OF THE CITY ALONG WITH THE ABANDONED IMMIGRANTS, EFFECTIVELY BLOCKING THE WATER-WAY AND CREATING A SEMI-FLOATING ISLAND. A STALEMATE, LOST PR BATTLE AND CITY-WIDE BUDGET CRISIS LED TO THE COUNCIL FINALLY DROPPING ALL DEMANDS.

OTHER CONTAINERS PAST THEIR PRIME ALSO BEGAN TO 'MYSTERIOUSLY WASH UP' NEXT TO THE ORIGINAL THREE. THE DECKS FORM THE UNSTABLE FOUNDATION FOR UNENDING TOWERS OF THESE LONG ABANDONED SHIPPING CONTAINERS, WHICH CREATE A HONEYCOMB-LIKE MICRO-CITY OF ITS OWN. THE ENTRANCE TO RIVERTOWN IS A TWENTY-FOOT WIDE METAL GRATE GANGPLANK THAT LEADS UP TO A ROUGH HOLE CUT INTO THE SIDE OF THE PING VENTURE TANKER. DUE TO ITS MAZE-LIKE DESIGN RIVERTOWN IS THE DARKEST SLUM IN PALOMAR CITY.

TO DATE RIVERTOWN IS NOT OFFICIALLY RECOGNIZED AS A DISTRICT AND IS THE ONLY SECTION OF THE CITY WITH ZERO LAW. NO POLICE, NO RECOGNIZED DISTRICT CRIME LORD, NO PROTECTION, EVERY MAN FOR HIMSELF. THIS IS THE LOWEST LEVEL OF PALOMAR'S CASTE.

PHOTO: D. CARDEZA / OBSERVER

CHARACTERS IN PALOMAR CITY

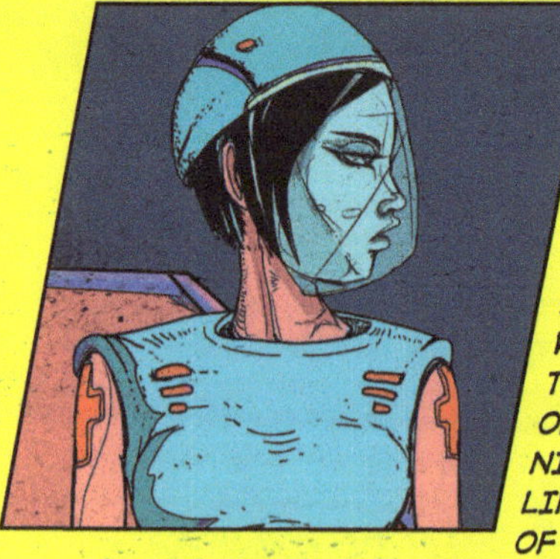

HEX SPENCER

HIXON "HEX" SPENCER IS A 25 YEAR-OLD FREELANCE MEDIC WHO WEARS TWO RED-CROSS TATTOOS ON BOTH OF HER SHOULDERS AND THE ATTITUDE OF A MARINE. HEX STARTED OUT AS PART OF A SOUGHT-AFTER COURIER TEAM, RUNNING ILLICIT WETWARE AROUND THE CITY FOR WHOMEVER WOULD PAY. AFTER A MYSTERIOUS RUN ENDS WITH THE DISAPPEARANCE OF HER SISTER, SHE'S LEFT HAVING TO TAKE CARE OF HER NIECE MELITA, AND REALIZES IT'S TIME TO RESET HER LIFE. GATECRASHING WAS A NATURAL FIT. HER KNOWLEDGE OF THE STREETS AND EXPERIENCE WITH WETWARE NETWORK MAKE HER ONE OF THE BEST GATECRASHERS AROUND – THOUGH THE FAST CASH OF THE WETWORK UNDERWORLD TEMPTS HER AT EVERY CORNER..

MELITA SPENCER

MELITA SPENCER IS HEX'S 13 YEAR-OLD NIECE. ABANDONED BY HEX'S OLDER SISTER UNDER MYSTERIOUS CIRCUMSTANCE, MELITA IS 2ND GENERATION GATES. BORN LONG AFTER THE CULTURE CLASHES, MELITA AND HER FRIENDS' WORLDS HAVE BEEN STRICTLY DEFINED BY THE GATES OF DISTRICT 11, BUT IT'S MELITA'S CURIOUSITY ABOUT THE DISSAPPEARANCE OF HER MOTHER THAT DRIVERS HER BEYOND THE GATES.

DETECTIVE THATCH

DETECTIVE THATCH IMMIGRATED TO PALOMAR CITY FROM CHINA IN 2034 WHEN HE WAS 19 YEARS OLD. ONCE A RISING STAR WITHIN THE PRESTIGIOUS STRC KIDNAP & RANSOM TASK FORCE, HE WAS RE-ASSIGNED TO THE PALOMAR PD VICE SQUAD IN THE POLITICAL FALLOUT FROM A MAJOR K&R CASE INVOLVING ONE OF PALOMAR CITY'S RICHEST FAMILIES. HE'S A GOOD MAN CAUGHT UP IN A CORRUPT SYSTEM.

DANE BRENNAN

DANE BRENNAN IS A FIFTH GENERATION OLIGARCH TO SHIPPING AND REAL ESTATE BEHEMOTH BRENNAN/STEINER. HOWEVER IT'S AT ONE'S OWN DETRIMENT TO UNDERESTIMATE HIM AS JUST A "SILVER SPOON". THE CONTINUAL DECAY OF THE CITY HAS MADE PORT MANAGEMENT A MORE DANGEROUS AND LUCRATIVE – JOB. SO DANE IS LOOKING FOR HIS NEXT MOVE TO CLAIM HIS PLACE IN THE FAMILY DYNASTY.

GUILLERMO CABALLERO

GUILLERMO CABALLERO WAS THE FIRST STREET SURGEON TO MAKE THE FLIP TO CRIME LORD. HE IS THE MEANEST OF THE MEAN AND THE MOST POWERFUL MAN IN DISTRICT 20. HIS LAIR IS THE HACIENDA, A MENACING MONOLITIC CITY-OF-A-BUILDING... A PLACE WHERE EVEN THE POLICE FEAR TO TREAD. FROM HIS PERCH ON THE TOP FLOOR CABALLERO HAS A CLEAR VIEW OF ALL OF PALOMAR CITY, AND A PLAN FOR ITS EVENTUAL TAKEOVER.

MAYOR GIRLIE WARREN

MAYOR GIRLIE WARREN HAD THE STRENGTH TO PULL HERSELF UP FROM THE SLUMS TO THE TIFFANY DISTRICTS, AND THE BALLS TO KICK ANYONE OUT OF HER WAY. AS THE NEWLY ELECTED MAYOR OF PALOMAR CITY, SHE IS AN IMELDA MARCOS TYPE FIGURE EQUAL PARTS LOVED AND DESPISED BY HER CONSTITUENCY. THERE ARE MANY ALLEGATIONS OF UNETHICAL ALLEGIANCES BETWEEN PALOMAR CITY POLITICIANS, TYCOONS AND INDUSTRIAL INTERESTS – IN PARTICULAR THE BRENNAN/STEINER DISTRICT 08 LUXURY TOWER ANNEXATION.

DR. OCTAVIO STAHL

DR. STAHL IS HEX'S MENTOR, A ONE-TIME GATECRASHER WHO LEARNED THE ROPES OF LIFE SAVING DURING THE CULTURE CLASHES, AND NOW TIRELESS DOCTOR IN PALOMAR GENERAL HOSPITAL. HE HAS DEDICATED HIS LIFE TO DOING THE RIGHT THING FOR ORDINARY PEOPLE, WHETHER OR NOT THE LAW IS ON HIS SIDE. HIS WORLD IS THE HELL IN THE HOSPITAL, NOT THE HELL ON THE STREETS.

ESTEFAN HAWK

ESTEFAN HAWK WAS BORN IN DISTRICT 11 ON APRIL 4, 1985, 5 YEARS AFTER THE TRAFFIC GATE SYSTEM WENT INTO EFFECT. FIRST GENERATION GATES (FIRST GEN) AND THE SON OF WORKING CLASS PARENTS, ESTEFAN WAS A STAR STUDENT, GRADUATING CUPC'S MEDICAL SCHOOL IN JUST THREE YEARS – ENTERING THE WORKFORCE IN 2017 JUST AFTER THE DISTRICT CULTURE CLASHES HIT THEIR PEAK. DUE TO CITY-WIDE TRAVEL RESTRICTIONS ESTEFAN FOUND HIMSELF PRIMARILY TREATING THE FOOT SOLDIERS OF DISTRICT 11, THEN RUN BY MR. STACY. HE CREATED THE FIRST RECOGNIZED WETWORK AND EVENTUALLY BECAME MR. STACY'S GO-TO SHOP FOR BODYMODS. UPON MR. STACY'S DEATH, ESTEFAN, NOW KNOWN AS "THE HAWK", TOOK OVER DISTRICT 11.

THE OBSERVER

PALOMAR CITY

IN THE DISTRICTS

AMBULANCES, SLEDS BY ANY OTHER NAME

PALOMAR CITY – Known by the Gatecrashers that drive them as sleds, ambulances evolved along with their duty. Every sled on the street has had a biometric ignition system since the Gates went into effect. Only the Gatecrashers can turn them on and drive them. These utilitarian vehicles underwent their biggest transformation during the Culture Clashes of the 2000's. Dispatchers added armor plating to fend off the continual pummeling by debris thrown from roofs and launched from makeshift canons and urban catapults. Years later as relative peace returned to the City, the armor became a functional anti-theft and vandalism device. Higher-end sleds have both reactive armor plates and retracting window and wheel coverage. When they stop, the entire body lurches with a loud grind n' clank, hydraulics hiss as reinforced door pistons jam into place and armored shields slide out to cover any glass while thick metal hoods drop over each tire. Most sleds have basic life support and medical facilities on board. Each two person crew has to pay for their own supplies, so they rarely keep much stock on hand.

TIFFANY CREWS

The regular Gatecrashers drive for an assortment of different dispatch companies, servicing a multitude of public hospitals. And then there are the Tiffany Crews. These private hospital ambulance teams operate more like black ops/special forces than medical staff. These guys don't fuck around. Their patients are the upper echelon of Palomar society and power (the people who don't mix with the PIM Eaters on the street). There is a long-standing rivalry between the Gatecrashers and the Tiffany Crews. They rarely cross paths, but the tension is palpable. On the odd occasion that a Gatecrasher picks up an insured private Drop, the Tiffany Crew will stop at nothing, including wrecking a rival sled, to retrieve their Drop. Tiffany Crews don't even let the often corrupt police get between them and a Drop. Cops know that they're no match for an insurance company's legal dept, so Tiffany Crews get away with murder – sometimes literally.

SKYNESTING SCOURGE

Factory owners in the mid 90's began to build skywards from the roofs of their factory buildings to create cheap, clandestine housing for migrant workers. This became known as Skynesting as the upper floors of buildings all over town started to resemble trees with clothes-lines, signs and decoration sprouting out of the windows of newly-erected levels.

But the architecture started to spin out of control. To accommodate additional labor flooding the City in record numbers, i.e. the Great Population Boom, brazen owners began to connect the tops of their buildings to neighboring buildings to take advantage of unused space. The practice continues unregulated and unabated today.

NO CHANGE AT PICCOLY / ROMY INDUSTRIES

It seems that the rumors of Piccoly/Romy spinning off their entertainment properties, including TELE7, RIBBA and WROT are being vehemently denied by the company shills. It is serious enough that they've even asked the caustic voice of the late-night airwaves, Billy Wood, to make a statement. Sounding more like a straight-laced suit than his usual loveable-asshole self, Wood stated, "I am very pleased with the resolution of my contract and I look forward to our new efforts to find synergy across all Piccoly/Romy industries."

Here at the Observer we are having a hard time seeing how Wood's slur-sploitation would find synergy in container ships, nuclear power, biomedical research and design. But I'm sure there's a good connection in there somewhere, one that we look forward to reporting on. In the mean time, don't miss RIBBA's show at the Romy Stadium.

BUSINESS

THE GATES: A BRIEF HISTORY

ARCHIVE: When the Gates were first installed in 1980, they were simple tollbooths manned by a new City department, the Traffic Response Control Unit (TRCU). These booths were quickly automated to allow for faster payment and traffic movement. As the City experienced an immense population explosion in the 1990's, traffic patterns began to focus on moving goods short distances to support the ever increasing population density. By the late 90's the Gates had returned to being manually operated by humans 24-hours a day.

Around the turn of the century, as civic unrest between Districts increased at a daily rate, walls and fences appeared, at times going up overnight. These unsanctioned structures were built primarily by District leaders using local funds. In 2003 when inter-district violence was at an all time high and City Hall could no longer ignore these structures, they responded by building a concrete mega-wall completely encircling District 05, home to the wealthy and City elite. The TRCU was assigned to all Gate Crossings and renamed Security Traffic Response Control Force – STRC (pronounced Strike) Force. This sent a definitive message to the population – keep to your own District. Within months the Culture Clashes were in full effect. With a shift to local governance of The Gate System in 2015, the gates/walls/fences/barriers/etc. all adapted to the specific needs of each District border. These Gates are more than psychological borders between commonly understood socio-political differences. Some Gates are heavily fortified, still manned 24 hours a day by STRC force personnel. Some sit empty, covered by posters, ads and flyers. Others have become outposts of criminals and graft.

The sole remaining continuity, shared by every Gate-crossing in Palomar City, is the Gatecrasher lane – reserved for medical emergency vehicles. The Gatecrasher lane is revered and protected by everyone from the most corrupt City politician to the most beneficent crime lord.

PIM RATES CLIMB

PALOMAR CITY – For the third quarter in a row, the base rate of domestically produced Protein Infused Meal [PIM] gained 1.3 percent to hit a 12-month high of US$10 per pound. Mayor Warren hinted at a possible food subsidy while the grain market is in turmoil.

THE RISE OF PIM

ARCHIVE – In 1990 as the Great Population Boom hit Palomar City, supplying food to the masses became increasingly difficult, with the street-dwellers taking the brunt of this shortfall. A black market for cheaply-imported and/or smuggled grain started new and more violent clashes and power struggles. In response, the City and Federal government initiated a plan to create the cheapest possible regulated "foodstuff". This was Protein Infused Meal, PIM, a tofu-like substance which could be eaten raw or cooked. This spawned an industry overnight. From street sales to fine dining PIM is the foundation of everyone's daily lives. PIM also successfully destroyed the food-smuggling industry, but made the City dependent on Government subsidized food.

VOICE OF THE STREET

Action 7's street team, headed by the lovely Charlotte P, uncovered a series of unlikely coincidences relating to the appropriation of City funds for Dock repairs in District 09. Charlotte's footage of Dane Brennan and Mayor Warren dining together in District 05 at Lucile's (see restaurant review in section D) caught what appears to be dock building plans tucked under Brennan's arm. As if the Brennan's didn't already control too much of Palomar City's waterways and commerce, it appears they want to raise the homes of thousands of PIM Eaters like you and me.

In more dock news, it's hard to miss the construction cranes rising above District 20. Our calls were not returned for comment by Hacienda honcho Guillermo Caballero, but there is definitely something underway on the waterfront. We'll be watching City Hall closely to see whether they'll start a war over permits or just stand by while another deathtrap rises above our skyline.

THE OBSERVER
PALOMAR CITY

METRO STYLE PAGES

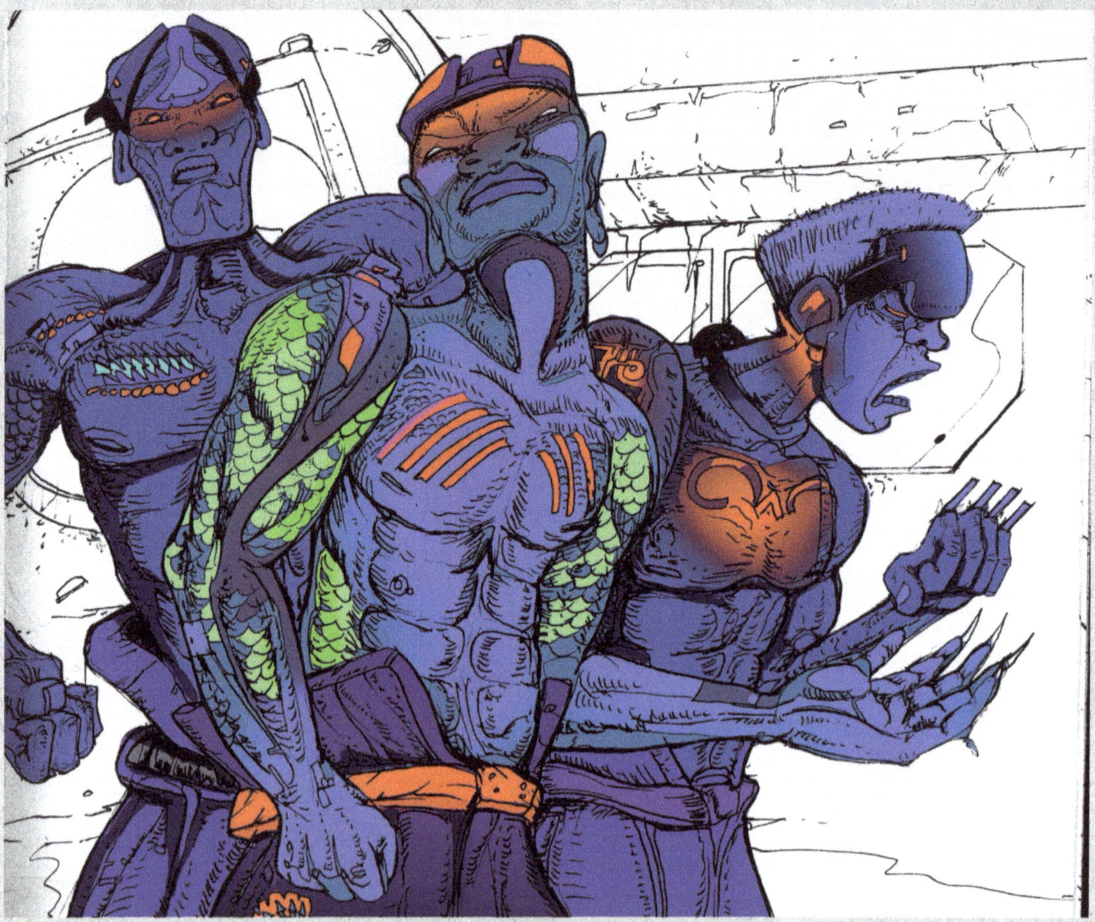

WETWORK: A BRIEF HISTORY

BY ELAINE VENTOU

Body Modification, commonly known as Wetwork for short – is a form of reconstructive surgery that evolved to a whole new level of medical interventi-ohn. Wetwork is the new class and the new ethnicity.

Think of Wetwork as an extension of extreme fashion - Harajuku kids meet Goth meet Heavy Metal meet Hip-Hop meet Skate. Then extend this mashup to tattoos and piercings. And then take it one step further to replacing eyes, limbs, skin, hair and anything else medically possible. Individual styles with very specific immediate meaning. In 2015 the first Wetwork started appearing on the street. A young doctor named Estefan Hawk, barely out of medical school, grafted experimental skin using rack-grown snake skin onto the forearms of three top gang leaders in District 11. The procedure was a success and it immediately became the ultimate status symbol in this tough gang-run District. Skins became the must have. And many other forms have followed.

METRO STYLE PAGES

WETWORK
THEN AND NOW

BY ELAINE VENTOU

SKINS

Then: The easiest and the first major Wetwork. Started with faux snake-skin and progressed to synthetics and many different polymers.

Now: Certain skins are reserved for gang members and leaders. These are the ultimate identifiers for different Districts.

STRAPS / CLAWS

Then: Muscle Strapping adds layer upon layer of rack-grown muscle to arms and legs. The rack-grown muscles are farmed in shops and buildings where they are pumped up on electrodes and fed with synthetic blood and PIM. "Claws" were born out of this. After a few years of perfecting the straps, it became popular to splice fingers together to support more hand muscle. This led to replacing bone with metal alloys, which made super-claws.

Now: Claws are out. That was a dying fad and claws are looked at as passé. Guys with claws are mostly the old-school thugs, lifer's that have been in for a long time. The younger set sees them as older and dumber.

SHADES / LENSES

Then: The first nano-fiber digital overlays were used to turn windows of airplanes and cars into data displays. Though eventually added to eye-glasses and sunglasses and ultimately to permanent contact lens systems, the interface still required a wired transceiver which snaked across and sometimes just under the skin and away from the eye. The next iteration of transceiver morphed into a sub-dermal micro-chip and is almost imperceptible.

Now: Current versions are two-way, with micro-lens that can record and broadcast. The lens is fitted on an antenna wire.

FINS

Then: Fins are thin metal pieces that began as purely decorative. Like the spines of a fish, usually running down and protruding from the outside of the forearm or across the top of the head like a Mohawk. Then they became controllable through muscle stimulus. Next they became reinforced to the bone and in extreme cases the bone replaced with metal alloys and so the spikes and fins became more lethal.

Now: The metal alloy bone replacement was outlawed by the City, which meant that anyone with Fins had to stay in Independent Districts. This has led to a proliferation and counter sub-culture of hidden fins and hidden blades.

SUB-DERMAL LED

Then: The origins of sub-dermal LED is unknown but thought to have been developed in clubs outside Rivertown, frequented by rich kids when that part of Palomar City was an abandoned warehouse area for late night vice. These small constellations of light on arms and foreheads has transformed into elaborate colors and full sheets of light. Also known as Lightware / Flashware / Lightshade / Flash.

Now: As Rivertown evolved into a closed society, its citizens have always been rumored to have adapted to their dark environment. The latest rumor (editor's note: unsubstantiated) is that their 'flash' is now all controlled by the user's thought, movement and environment.

Where did the idea for The Gatecrashers come from?

The idea started with health insurance. , a very sexy beginning to any good adventure. At the time I didn't have any and I was trying to figure out how to get covered. The health insurance industry was a disaster and for a young freelancer it was beyond hope (maybe still is). Also, living in New York City I've taken a cab to a hospital a few times and those experiences got me thinking, 'Just how different would it be if ambulance drivers were more like cabbies?' What would it take to get us to that point? So I created Palomar City, a near future American mega-city – imagined like a New York City, quadrupled in population within the same physical space. This isn't a post-apocalyptic dystopian future, it's a real future of continued financial prosperity and the evolution of global migration and the further divide between the rich and the poor.

Then I was back to thinking about those ambulance teams, who would they be and how much training might they need? I arrived at a cross between a bike messenger, slipping in and out of super-congested city-traffic, and cabbies who have to pay a rental fee on their vehicles, work 12 hour shifts, get a cursory license, report to dispatchers and get paid based on how many fares they pick up.

For a time the project was just called Ambulance, I was looking for a better title and the word Gatecrasher caught my eye. Using the word Gatecrasher the idea of the Gates was born. This allowed me to divide the city up, further segregate it, forcing those new populations into ever smaller spaces known as Districts, which in turn created a new social structure where not all citizens can travel freely. This gave the ambulance teams something that really sets them apart from the other citizens - a free pass to roam the city.

There are a few cities that have created zoned traffic systems for their urban centers, London and Stockholm being two high profile and successful ones. A few years ago, Mayor Bloomberg was pushing for this in New York, but he couldn't get it through. (so he closed down a lot of streets, turned them into pedestrian plazas and added tons of bike lanes, which was awesome). I thought, what if a city had tried this in the early 1980's and the technology of that era would have necessitated physical toll booths. So the city installs these toll booths at major street crossings in and out of various neighborhoods. And, as happens with so many civil infrastructure projects, it doesn't age well. Twenty years on the tolls barely pay for themselves and the least used booths start to get decommissioned by the city - taken over as newspaper and cigarette kiosks and creating new physical neighborhood borders.

photo: Bob Jones

First the population boom begins. An inspiration for the population boom was an amazing article by Patrick Radden Keefe in the New Yorker. He details the Snakehead industry, the smuggling of Chinese immigrants, and a major event that shined light on it which was the Golden Venture ship running aground in Sheepshead Bay, New York.

"According to Peter Kwong, a professor at Hunter College and an authority on American Chinatowns, the largest influx of illegal Chinese in the country's history entered the United States between 1988 and 1993. A United Nations study estimated that by the mid-nineties the snakehead trade from China to the United States was a three-and-a-half-billion-dollar industry." - *New Yorker* **The Snakehead**

There is another great article that pushed this idea for me, *A Letter From Sao Paulo: City of Fear* by William Langewiesche. In it he describes local gangs so powerful that they shut down City Hall. These same gangs that migrated out of prisons, essentially create small local governments and do a better job (certainly up for debate as they rule with violence and crime) than the corrupt police and politicians. Law abiding citizens support a criminal they trust over a politician they don't. So the crime lords rise to the top. Sao Paolo is the largest city in South America with a population of 20 million people. It is home to international banks and businesses, glass skyscrapers and some of Brazil's wealthiest people. But it also has a massive population, millions by most accounts, living in Favelas which are shantytowns and slums. They are built with illegal construction on land appropriated, not bought. These two populations co-exist with an undeniable tension, and all this is happening in an internationally thriving metropolis.

This is Palomar City.

So in this world we now have these toll gates defining neighborhoods and more and more people moving in creating cultural concentrations that have led to violent culture clashes. These riots and violence are inspired by the Bombay Riots of 1992. But in the fictional world of Palomar City, I imagine that their anger is directed not just at their neighbors but at City Hall whose apathy is increasing toward the underprivileged and immigrant communities. This would look something like Occupy Wall Street. I can imagine a time when a city government is so bankrupt financially and politically that they basically give up. This doesn't happen overnight, it takes years of turmoil, violence, hundreds of millions of dollars in increased police and military efforts. Then finally a Mayor looks at the situation and realizes that they have not been in control of certain neighborhoods for 20 years, no taxes are being paid, no police patrol those streets any longer and he simply says, "If you think you can run the city better, go for it, District 10 is yours." So District 10 becomes an independent city state and soon many more follow.

In book one of "A Night Of Gatecrashing" that sets up some of the characters and the world, we decided to depict the gates and walls as much larger, more substantial, but that is not how they started. They were originally just toll booths. Then during the culture clashes different neighborhoods began to create makeshift barricades, built out of car parts, wood scraps, chain link stolen from city parks and all this connected buildings to the toll booths to define their turf. After a few years of trying to fight this, city hall finally built their own walls between the richest districts and their neighboring independent ones. Over the next twenty years as the walls and gates became a way of life, the walls multiplied and people stopped even noticing them for what they were.

What are your literary or Media influences and Inspirations?

William Gibson is without a doubt at the top of my list of the best science fiction, hands down. "Neuromancer" and "Burning Chrome" are books I could pick up any day of the week and just start reading. Yes, there are unabashed appropriations, allusions and homages to Gibson's work in The Gatecrashers, though I'd venture to say the near future he envisioned has become a reality, and the future I'm envisioning is built on top of that reality. The internet and even You-tube make a debut in "Neuormancer." How can those realities not be weaved into the new future?

My more contemporary influences are HBO's "The Wire" and also "A Song of Ice and Fire" ("Game of Thrones") books by George R.R. Martin. Both of those storyworlds transcend their genre to be about society. "The Wire" with a tight focus on one city, Baltimore, and Game of Thrones' which encompasses a fictitious Europe, the Mediterranean and the Middle East. But whether it is swords and dragons or burners and police surveillance, it's the inner-workings of a complete society that make those stories interesting. It isn't one character so much as it's all of them at once. However the world is the biggest character of all and I could only hope to accomplish something as awesome as either of those storyworlds.

What are some defining characteristics of the people who live in Palomar City?

For the most part the citizens of Palomar City are a lot like you and me. They have to go to work, pay rent, do homework...basically live life while engaged in the daily grind.

But, one big difference in this world is the proliferation and value of Wetwork, aka body modification. Wetwork will only continue to get more extreme. Right now, in the world we live in, the most invasive of body modification is intended to be indistinguishable, nose jobs, boob jobs, nips, tucks, lifts. The least invasive is meant to radically change your appearance, tattoos, piercings, spacers and more.

Street-level walk-in plastic surgery stores were unheard of a mere 20 years ago. But now they exist in central and South America. So it's not a stretch that cosmetic surgery will attain a level of acceptability and people will change it up with a regularity that the change in seasonal fashions enjoy today. And I think it's safe to assume that some of the tech MIT is currently developing will be appropriated away from making thought controlled artificial hands, to thought controlled personal horns or fins. In our world there will be the street level hijacked tech as well as the Haute Couture of tech available only to the rich. And aspirational tech transcends all strata of society.

There will be those who will always be trying to get their hands on it. Street-level wetwork will be the equivalent of counterfeit Gucci handbags - only instead of fake leather it'll be cheap fake rack-grown muscle instead of high-end graft work. But with the ever-increasing progress of neuro-controlled artificial limbs as well as societie's fascination with adornment - piercing, tattoos and colored contacts - cosmetic surgery and fashion will collide and that's the future our wetwork lives in.

As wearables turn into implants, wetwork will become real and as it does, those fashion statements will come to represent neighborhoods and wetwork could supplant ethnicity and social identity.

Where Is the Federal Government in all this?

By 2045 we will have seen states secede from the union. Idaho, Montana and Texas will be nation states and god knows their borders will be closed and trespassers shot on sight.

A few hundred thousand people declaring succession and cramming themselves into a few square miles of a shitty, dirty, exciting, hedonistic, cultural, international business-center? The federal government is going to do their best to keep that concept from spreading, but they'll leave Palomar City alone. It has always been a bit of a unique American city that the rest of the country just doesn't get, but surely wants to visit and party there.

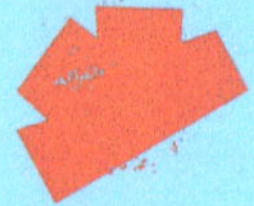

THE TEAM

ZACHARY MORTENSEN // CREATOR / WRITER

Zach is founder of Ghost Robot, a New York City based creative production company. He has produced feature films such as First Winter and Creative Control, both by Benjamin Dickinson, Peter Callahan's Against The Current and Steve Barron's Choking Man. His documentaries include Cropsey by Joshua Zeman and Barbara Brancaccio, George Ratliff's Hell House and Sara Lamm's Dr. Bronner's Magic Soapbox and Birth Story: Ina May Gaskin & The Farm Midwives. With Ghost Robot, Zach is constantly producing commercials, music videos and branded content, recent clients include: Nike, Ford, United Airlines, Verizon, Microsoft, Puma and Dos XX as well as music videos and short films for artists like Reggie Watts, Michael Cera, AIR, Bjork, Killer Mike, Diane Birch, and Yoko Ono.

SUTU // ARTIST

Sutu is an international award winning illustrator, writer and interactive designer. He is best known for being the creator of NAWLZ - a 24 episode online interactive cyberpunk series and NEOMAD, a three part space opera set in the Australian outback. Sutu has also adapted traditional Australian Aboriginal stories into interactivestorybooks for iPad. His work has been exhibited both nationally and internationally including a solo exhibition as a part of the Bucheon International Comic festival in Seoul, South Korea.

DIANA WILLIAMS // EDITOR / PRODUCER

Diana is the founder of Roller Coaster Entertainment. With experience in production, IP creation and multi-platform stragegy, Diana has produced features and television (Our Song, Gun Hill, ILM: Creating the Impossible), comic book adaptations (Peter Panzer-faust, Broken Girls), animation (Tron: Legacy, Torchwood: Web of Lies), webseries (Awesome Asian Bad Guys, Chinafornia) and consulted on the award-winning documentary Room 237 and The Digits, a cross-platform interactive narrative webseries and math app "Fraction Blast". Currently diana is the producer of content strategy for Lucasfilm.

explore the world

TheGatecrashers.com

ghostrobot   THE GATECRASHERS

A NIGHT OF GATECRASHING
BOOK ONE

www.ingramcontent.com/pod-product-compliance
Lightning Source LLC
Chambersburg PA
CBHW041209100726
47911CB00017B/905